SWEET PLUMERIA DAWN

MAUI ISLAND SERIES BOOK 6

KELLIE COATES GILBERT

Copyright © 2022 by Kellie Coates Gilbert

All rights reserved.

No part of this book may be reproduced in any form or by any electronic or mechanical means, including information storage and retrieval systems, without written permission from the author, except for the use of brief quotations in a book review.

Sweet Plumeria Dawn is a work of fiction. Names, characters, places, and incidents are either the product of the author's imagination or are used fictitiously, and any resemblance to actual persons, living or dead, is coincidental.

Cover Design: Elizabeth Mackay

*For Joyce Carol Mintzas,
A treasured reader who sets everything aside to read preview copies
of my books before publication*

PRAISE FOR KELLIE COATES GILBERT

"If you're looking for a new author to read, you can't go wrong with Kellie Coates Gilbert."
~**Lisa Wingate**, NY Times bestselling author of *Before We Were Yours*

"Well-drawn, sympathetic characters and graceful language"
~**Library Journal**

"Deft, crisp storytelling"
~**RT Book Reviews**

"I devoured the book in one sitting."
~**Chick Lit Central**

"Gilbert's heartfelt fiction is always a pleasure to read."
~**Buzzing About Books**

"Kellie Coates Gilbert delivers emotionally gripping plots and authentic characters."
~**Life Is Story**

"I laughed, I cried, I wanted to throw my book against the wall, but I couldn't quit reading.
~**Amazon reader**

"I have read other books I had a hard time putting down, but this story totally captivated me."

~**Goodreads reader**

"I became somewhat depressed when the story actually ended. I wanted more."
~**Barnes and Noble reader**

ALSO BY KELLIE COATES GILBERT

THE MAUI ISLAND SERIES
Under The Maui Sky

Silver Island Moon

Tides of Paradise

The Last Aloha

Ohana Sunrise

Sweet Plumeria Dawn

Songs of the Rainbow

Hibiscus Christmas

THE PACIFIC BAY SERIES
Chances Are

Remember Us

Chasing Wind

Between Rains

THE SUN VALLEY SERIES
Sisters

Heartbeats

Changes

Promises

LOVE ON VACATION SERIES

Otherwise Engaged

All Fore Love

TEXAS GOLD SERIES

A Woman of Fortune

Where Rivers Part

A Reason to Stay

What Matters Most

STAND ALONE NOVELS

Mother of Pearl

* * *

Available at all retailers

www.kelliecoatesgilbert.com

SWEET PLUMERIA DAWN
MAUI ISLAND SERIES, BOOK 6

Kellie Coates Gilbert

1

There were few things Ava Briscoe enjoyed more than family gatherings, even those that held a bit of mystery.

Two days ago, Vanessa showed up at her door with a request. That alone was not unusual. Her sister typically had a long list of ways others could meet her needs, wishes, and desires. Vanessa was the epitome of a globe head—someone who believed the entire world revolved around her.

Ava had learned to brace herself with each encounter, no matter how brief. Yet nothing had prepared her for this new bombshell surprise.

Vanessa tossed her Louis Vuitton on the counter and helped herself to a bottle of sparkling water from Ava's refrigerator. "Okay, here's the deal," she said. "I want the entire family to come over tomorrow night. I have an announcement."

Ava hoped her sister had found a new job. It had been nearly a month since she'd been suddenly terminated from her position as Communications Director and Media Liaison for Jim Kahele's state senator campaign.

Okay, termination might not be the right word. Vanessa had

quit. Her pride couldn't handle what she considered a demotion after Jim hired a beautiful young woman and made her Campaign Manager. "I'll never work for that bimbo," she'd claimed. "He thinks I'll report to his girlfriend? Well, he's dead sorry wrong on that assumption. That's just nepotism. I won't have it." Never mind that she, too, had dated Jim before going to work for him.

The entire scenario painted a new perspective on Vanessa's campaign slogan—Your Choice for Change.

Truthfully, Ava was saddened to learn Vanessa had lost her dream job. It was not the first time. Months back, her sister had landed on Maui after being asked to vacate her anchor desk at a big news station in Seattle for making a political snafu on air. She loved that job, and she was good at it. Her ability to spin a story and wheedle people into her camp was unsurpassed, which was another reason Jim's offer to join his campaign had been right up her alley. Vanessa joked that political campaigning was nothing more than promising to build a bridge, even when there was no river.

Ava leaned against the kitchen counter. "Care to give me a preview of the big announcement?" she asked.

Vanessa vehemently shook her head. "No. It's a surprise. A big one."

Ava folded. Despite the heavy schedule at Pali Maui and the short notice, she had no choice but to go along with her sister's proposal. Not unless she wanted to engage in an argument. "Okay, but I can't promise everyone will be able to make it. You will have to make all the calls because I'm tight on time. We have an important meeting today with an advertising agency. Christel and I decided to explore venturing into a new international social media campaign. The agency promises they can increase our revenues by fifty percent...ambitious in my opinion, but Christel believes we need to hear what they have to say."

"Absolutely," Vanessa agreed. "If you're unwilling to plunge forward and embrace new ways of doing things, you will fall victim to lagging behind."

To her surprise, the party came together, and everyone was in attendance except Katie's husband, Jon. It was rare that he could leave No Ka 'Oi during the heavy dinner hour. Even on weeknights, his restaurant overlooking the golf course at Pali Maui was booked to capacity. He did promise to have the cooks prepare extra entrées and have Katie deliver them to save Ava needing to prepare food for the get-together. Her son-in-law was thoughtful like that.

Katie was the first to arrive with her teen daughter, Willa, and little Noelle. "So, what is Aunt Vanessa's big news?" she asked while unloading the food.

Ava lifted a box out of Katie's trunk. "I have absolutely no idea." She sniffed the aroma wafting from the closed lid. "Mmm...smells delicious."

"Hamachi tacos. Jon lifted the recipe from Morimoto's menu on their website," she confided. "He duplicated the dish to a tee."

Noelle lifted her chubby little arm in the air. "Me want a taco. Me want a taco."

Katie gave her a patient look. "You have to wait for dinner, sweetheart." She performed a typical mommy maneuver to stave off a meltdown and offered her a substitute. "You can have some pineapple. Maybe Grammy Ava has a little chocolate syrup you can dip the pieces in."

"That sounds healthy," Ava teased.

"Healthy is overrated," Willa chimed in. "Take it from me; you do not want this little girl having a tantrum when she's hungry."

Ava wondered why Katie couldn't simply let her little daughter eat an early dinner, though she didn't say it. She'd learned long ago not to meddle in her adult children's decisions. If she'd done her job and raised them properly, they would make good choices on all the essential things.

Shane was a perfect example. Who would have thought her wild child would embrace the unexpected responsibilities laid at his feet when Aimee showed up at his door with a surprise son? Or, when she flew back to the mainland a short time later, leaving little Carson and a simple note on the counter with little explanation for her sudden departure beyond wanting to make it big in Hollywood?

Her son had stepped up. He'd sold his motorcycle and left his all-nighters behind to be there for his precious little son, validating her adage even more.

All of her kids were proof that good parenting and putting your children first often panned out.

That didn't mean she still didn't have concerns for her children. At times, she worried about Aiden. He was a perfectionist, never allowing himself any latitude to fail. Since his promotion to chief at the rescue station, those tendencies had magnified. This left little room for a social life. Outside the family and an occasional surfing excursion, her son rarely made time for fun.

The doorbell rang, and Ava moved to answer. It was Christel and Evan. "Hi, sweetheart." Ava pulled her oldest daughter into a hug, then turned and embraced her son-in-law. "How are things?" she asked, trying to mask the real question that had been looming month after month for a while now.

Christel and Evan were desperately trying to get pregnant but had put the attempt on hold because of the stress it caused Christel. Her oldest daughter was another one who never allowed herself to fall short on any level. Her girl was prone to being a little high-strung, had made the Dean's List multiple times at Loyola Law School in Chicago, and got her law and CPA licenses, all so she could run the legal and financial aspects of Pali Maui. No slacking with that girl.

Rarely did Christel fail at anything. Ava's heart broke to

know her daughter struggled with her inability to become pregnant. Especially since she'd wanted a family when she married Jay. The heartbreak of his addiction and the divorce robbed her of so much, including time.

Ava suspected Christel's age might be contributing to her difficulties in the child-bearing department. Still, as the fertility expert had reported, Christel was not too old, and there were no physical findings that would preclude her from pregnancy.

Her friend, Alani, claimed babies were a gift from God. It would happen, in His time.

Her brother, Jack, was the next to arrive. He came bringing a gift...a bottle of his favorite rum. "So, what's the occasion?" he asked, balancing his unlit cigar between his lips.

Ava drew him into the living area to join the others. "Vanessa has a surprise announcement."

Her sister clapped her hands with excitement. "Yes, I do."

When everyone had arrived, Ava motioned for her family to take seats around the large dining table in the adjoining room. "I hope everyone's hungry."

They were all gathered, ready to dig into Jon's delicious food when Vanessa could stand it no longer. She stood and clinked a knife against her water goblet.

"Listen up. It's time for me to share my big news, everyone."

She paused, waiting for everyone's eyes to be directed her way. She loved to be the center of attraction, and tonight was no exception.

Willa lifted the taco from her plate. "So, what's the big announcement, Aunt Vanessa?"

Vanessa paused to stretch the building of anticipation. Finally, she let her face break into a wide smile. She clasped her hands together, giddy with excitement.

"This morning, I filed my paperwork to run for office, beginning my candidacy. I'm going to run against Jim Kahale and become Hawaii's next state senator!"

2

Christel pulled two large cardboard boxes from the trunk of her car and carried them inside. Without stopping to answer her buzzing phone, she headed for the spare bedroom and tossed the boxes on the thick, carpeted floor before turning her attention to the items on the bed.

She'd been struggling for several weeks. Aunt Vanessa's news about her decision to run for state senator had been the frosting on the wilting cupcake.

Her aunt was jumping off the proverbial cliff into the political arena...not just in a support role, but as a candidate.

Christel was frankly jealous.

Issues mattered to Christel...the environment and climate, racial equity, shifting the tax burden onto the one percent, and massive tech corporations that rarely paid their fair share. Her views were not shared by the rest of her family, especially her mom. Her family learned to refrain from political discussions, which often ended in misunderstandings and arguments. Still, getting involved at a much deeper level had always played in the back of her mind, and she'd neglected that dream.

Now, Aunt Vanessa was walking the journey she thought she'd take someday...and with stilettos. Her aunt did everything with style.

Life was full of choices. She liked to believe she'd made the right ones—still, the road not taken beckoned when she heard Aunt Vanessa's announcement.

Not that Christel was a sloucher. Just the opposite.

Christel's list of successes was long. She'd carefully mapped her life out from the time she was in high school. With few exceptions, she'd accomplished each of her goals.

Graduated high school with full-ride scholarship offers to multiple prestigious schools...check.

Completed a four-year business program at the University of California, Berkeley in three years...check.

Made dean's list at Loyola School of Law and graduated with high honors...check.

At the end of that same summer, she passed the bar first try...check.

Studied and passed the CPA exam two months later...check.

Joined her family business and became a respected force in the business community, not only in Hawaii but internationally...check.

Yes, there were many items on her success list. Yet, there were also failures.

Her crumbled marriage to Jay was the most significant. Her inability to sway him from abusing alcohol landed her face-to-face with the fact that not everything was in her control. You could do everything right and still lose.

Now, she had to add failing to get pregnant. Another undertaking that seemed entirely out of her control. Or, maybe something inside her wasn't as ready to be a mother as she'd thought, and her body was telling her so.

Christel sighed, lifted the tiny onesie with the printed bunnies off the bed, and carefully folded it. She brought the little garment to her nose and sniffed the powdery smell baby items seemed to carry before placing it in the box. Next, she folded the pretty pink gown and the light blue jumpsuit...proof she didn't care whether she had a boy or girl. Ten fingers and ten toes would be enough.

The items went in the box next to the onesie.

Christel had just finished packing the items when she heard the front door close.

"Christel? You home?"

"I'm in here, Evan." She quickly closed the lid on the box and shoved it aside. She lifted from where she sat on the bed and brushed off her hands on her pants.

"What are you doing home so early?" Her husband leaned against the door jamb with his arms crossed. "I thought you said you had meetings all day."

Christel tucked a stray piece of hair behind her ear. "I did. The last one was rescheduled at the last minute. Something about the supplier forgetting he had a school thing he needed to attend for his daughter."

Evan nodded. "Got to admire priorities." He moved inside the room and placed a kiss on Christel's forehead. "Do we have dinner plans?"

Christel cringed. "No. *We* didn't put anything out to thaw."

From the look on her husband's face, her comment hit the mark intended. As was Evan's style, he didn't engage. Her husband detested unnecessary conflict. "No problem. Do you want me to go pick something up?"

He'd had three surgeries that day and had to be exhausted. "No, I'll do it," she told him.

"What's the box?"

She glanced over her shoulder. "What box?"

Evan let out a laugh. "The one you are looking at?"

"Oh...I'm just packing up a few things."

Evan's eyebrows raised. "The things that were laid out on the bed? The baby things?"

Christel drew a breath and extracted herself from her husband's examination. "Yes. I thought it best if we put them away until...if I get pregnant."

"So, you're not..."

Christel shook her head. "No." Another month. Another negative test.

She went to move past him, but he caught her shoulders.

"Honey, it will happen."

His empty promise did nothing to sway her internal doubt. Still, she nodded. "Yeah, I know."

"We could always..."

She quickly held up her hand against what she knew was coming. "We discussed this."

He nodded in resignation, then rubbed the back of his neck with his hand. "Why don't we just order some pizza? We're both tired."

Christel turned for the door, knowing he watched her. "Sure. I'm up for whatever you want." The disappointment that remained painted on her husband's face prompted her to add, "Next month, Evan. I'm sure it'll happen next month."

It was the most naked statement that wasn't true she'd ever spoken to him.

3

Aiden shifted the six-pack of beer under his arm and rang his brother's doorbell. When there was no answer, he rang again. Still no response, so he wandered to the window and peered inside to find his brother crashed out on the sofa, sound asleep.

Aiden hesitated a few minutes before he shrugged and returned to the door. He pounded on the wood.

A few seconds passed, and he pounded again.

"Okay, okay…I'm coming!"

More noise came from inside. The door finally opened, and Shane stood there wearing his pants with no shirt. His hair was sticking up in several directions. His belt was undone, and one end hung at his knees. "Sorry, man. I must've dozed off."

Aiden tousled his younger brother's hair. "Dozed? I'd say you were out for the count, bro."

Shane looked at him, irritated at having been woken from a deep sleep. "Hey, quit throwing shade. You try being up all night with a kid who has his internal clock all messed up. I mean, it's four o'clock in the morning, and Carson decides it's time to play. He's learned to say Da-Da. It was cute at first…but repeated non-stop in the middle of the night gets old, really quick."

Aiden laughed. "Ha...there was a time not so long ago when you never even went to bed until after four in the morning. You're getting soft, little brother."

Shane landed a playful punch against Aiden's shoulder. "At least I was a player. You, my friend, not so much."

"What do you mean?"

"Mom flies off to the east coast with her new boyfriend. Christel has a surprise wedding. Katie and Jon still sneak off to spend afternoons alone in their new house. While I don't currently have anyone in the picture, Carson proves I wasn't afraid to take a risk. I'm just slowing down for a bit...temporarily."

"And you think I'm afraid to take a risk?" Aiden shook his head vehemently. "I'm just selective. Not interested in anyone with nothing but air between the ears."

Shane grabbed one of the beers from its plastic pack ring. "When was the last time you kissed a girl, bro? Or even dated one, for that matter?" He popped the tab on the top of the can and lifted it to his mouth.

Aiden slid into a barstool and set the rest of the beer cans on the marble countertop. "I date."

Shane shook his head, failing to hold back his laughter. "Oh really? What was her name?" His eyes grew wide. "Oh, wait. Maybe you're..." He didn't finish his sentence. Instead, he tilted his palm back and forth.

Aiden sighed with disgust. "Whether I like guys or girls is not at issue. Geez, what's with you?"

His brother shrugged. "I'm just saying. I mean, that girl you work with is hot. What about her?"

"Megan McCord? She's an employee."

"So?"

"So, you don't get romantically involved with people you

supervise," he pointed out.

"Tell that to Aunt Vanessa." Shane tossed his empty can in the sink and grabbed another.

Aiden scowled at the fresh can in his brother's hand. "I see you haven't slowed down on everything."

"I'm rehydrating after being up all night."

Aiden could argue that alcohol dehydrated the system and explain the physiology of his reasoning, but why invite more disdain? Shane already believed he was a wonk...at least in the romance department.

That wasn't so far from the truth. It'd been over a year since he'd even been remotely interested in anyone. In his defense, his promotion had consumed all of his attention and time. Suddenly finding yourself thrust into a position of immense responsibility came with repercussions.

Shane stood and did up his belt. "Well, buddy. I've got your back."

"What do you mean?"

"I mean, I made some arrangements."

Aiden groaned. "Oh no." He shook his head. "I don't like where this is going. What arrangements?"

"You'll see," his brother told him. "Just be here tomorrow night at seven. Willa has agreed to babysit. You and I are going out on the town...with some friends."

"What friends?"

"Never you mind. Just wear some aftershave, and I promise you'll go home with a smile on your face."

KATIE LEANED against a stack of pillows and drummed her fingers on the bed covers. The clock on her nightstand reflected that Jon was late getting home. The restaurant had been closed for over two hours. She reached for her phone to call and see what was up when she heard his car pull into the drive.

The sound brought a smile to her face. It'd been weeks since she and Jon had enjoyed any amorous activity, and she planned to end that streak tonight. If she got her way, morning would not dawn without serious marital action between the clean sheets she put on the bed this afternoon.

Katie smoothed her new nightgown, imagining it crumpled on the floor after Jon caught on to her plans. She fully intended to get noisy, which made her very glad she designed this house with the girls' bedrooms a good distance from their own.

When Jon finally showed up in the doorway, Katie donned her sexiest smile and opened the bed covers in a not-so-hidden invitation to join her. "Hi, Babe."

Jon took one look and groaned. "Oh, honey. Not tonight. I'm seriously exhausted. We had the dinner party from hell tonight. They sent every entrée back to the kitchen. Every single one."

"Sent them back?" She sat up in bed, angry at those horrid people who had deflated her plans. "Why?"

"They claimed the shitake puffed pastry bouchée was flavorless. The shrimp bisque was too strongly seasoned. The fish dumplings in sorrel sauce came out too doughy.

Katie scowled. "And you let them?"

Jon unbuttoned his shirt. "Let them?"

"Yeah. One return might slide but sending all the entrées back to the kitchen doesn't pass the "Karen" test."

Jon pulled his shirt off and tossed it over a chair. "Not following."

"The "Karen" test. Don't you watch Tik-Tok?"

Her husband shook his head. "Afraid not. When do I have time?"

Katie crossed her arms across her chest. "You have to stand up to those kinds of people, Jon. For goodness sake, you got taken tonight. Sent down the proverbial reprehensible customer river."

"Really? What would you have had me do, Katie? Refuse them?"

"Yes, refuse them. They ordered. They eat. They pay." Her jaw set. "I bet they ate half their meal before claiming there were issues. Am I right?"

Jon waved off her concerns. "Look, it's over. Let's just get to bed. I'm beat."

Katie relented. She'd take up this conversation tomorrow. She knew Jon wouldn't hear any of her concerns and wouldn't take her seriously when he was tired. Neither would he participate in any of her plans for sex.

She sighed. "Okay, but this is not over, Jon. Seriously."

In a matter of minutes after his head hit the pillow, his snores filled the room.

Katie turned over and beat her pillow into submission before repositioning her head. She wished she could follow suit and doze off, but her mind whirled.

She'd offered hundreds of times to help Jon at the restaurant. He always declined. "We're better off not working together, honey. I mean, seriously. We'd end up butting heads every day."

Katie sighed, knowing that was true. More, she didn't even want to help at the restaurant. Not really.

The truth was, she needed a new project. The Concerts at Pali Maui were now a thing…a very successful thing. Residents and tourists across the island enjoyed the venue and all it had to offer. Music, great food, and an opportunity to spread a blanket and chill while enjoying an evening with friends and family.

Sadly, there was little effort on her part remaining. She had pulled all her plans off beautifully. Except for a few hours a week, the concerts nearly ran themselves.

Same with the gift shop and tour bus. Her inventory orders were primarily made quarterly, and the tours took very little of her time and attention.

She needed something new...something that would pique her interest and give her a reason to get out of bed in the morning filled with enthusiasm. It wasn't like she could build another house.

That's when the idea hit her.

Aunt Vanessa was running to be the state's new senator. Surely, she'd need help. Someone with a penchant for new ideas and the ability to roll up her sleeves and execute those plans would be essential.

Katie picked up her phone and quickly typed out a text. She pushed send, clicked off the bedside lamp, then slid deep inside the covers with a broad smile on her face.

Her head was already brimming with possibilities.

4

"Where are we going?" Alani flipped the car visor down and gazed at her reflection in the small mirror. "You know, I like this new one."

"I agree. The new wig looks great. How many do you have now?"

Alani's cheeks blushed as she answered. "I lost count. Even though my hair is growing back, I don't seem able to quit buying new ones. Who wants to take the time to fuss with your hair when you can slip on the latest style in a matter of minutes?"

Ava grinned, happy that her friend had finally turned the corner on her illness. "You deserve any number of wigs after all you've been through. It's no secret that Elta and I both suffered moments of wondering what the future held."

Alani waved her off. "There's no need to worry when you know your future is in the hands of God. My pastor husband should know that. And, you..." She paused and pointed her finger in Ava's direction. "You get a pass, but only because I couldn't have made it through cancer without all your support."

Her eyes turned a little teary. "You certainly earned your angel wings, my friend."

Ava pulled into a parking spot and cut the engine. "So did your kids."

Alani smiled. "Yes, they both stepped up and were there for Elta and me. Especially Mia."

"Is she staying?"

Alani nodded. "I think so. My girl has made great strides in forgiving herself for what she did to you and your family." She reached for Ava's hand. "Thanks to you. I will never tire of telling you how much it meant to me that you were willing to forgive her. While the relationship will never be the same after her affair with Lincoln, the power of her horrid choices was greatly diminished. Ultimately, evil did not win."

Ava swallowed. Despite the choice to move on and live with joy, emotion would always threaten to pull her under whenever she was reminded of her husband's infidelity and the hurt. It was the only thing she was not completely honest about with her best friend. No good came from pulling Alani's spirits down with her own, especially when all of Alani's attention needed to be directed to beating a potentially fatal illness.

She forced a smile. "I have too much to be grateful for to wallow in the past." She patted her friend's knee.

Alani looked around with curiosity. "Why are we at the Shops at Wailea? You didn't say we were going shopping today."

Ava pointed to a second-floor door in a building located in the retail center. "We're not. We're visiting my sister's new campaign office."

"What? They moved Jim Kahale's office?"

Ava shook her head. "Not exactly."

"Not following you."

Ava motioned for Alani to get out of the car. "You'll see."

They rode the elevator to the second floor. Alani's eyes went wide when the doors opened, and they stepped out. She stepped closer to the large brass nameplate on the door flanked with red, white, and blue bunting. "Vanessa is running for office? Our Vanessa?"

Ava nodded. "Yes, it appears that way." She quickly explained about Vanessa's perceived demotion when her former love-interest-turned-candidate hired his new girlfriend and made her campaign manager. "There's no one more ambitious than a woman scorned," she told her friend.

"There's no one more ambitious than your sister," Alani muttered as she peeked through the glass sidelight to the right of the entry.

Before Ava could place her hand on the knob, the door flung open. Vanessa stood there, ready to greet them with a wide smile. "Welcome to my new campaign headquarters!" She waved them inside. "We're not quite finished setting up, but my amazing team has us nearly there."

A young guy wearing a T-shirt knelt near a wall. He held a screwdriver in one hand and a long black cord in the other. "Hey," he said in greeting.

"That's Kickback," Vanessa explained.

Alani's eyes went wide. "The guy who made a name for himself riding Jaws?"

Vanessa nodded. "Yes. We extended an offer and were lucky he decided to join my team."

The kid grinned. "I was a volunteer for Jim. She offered a salary. No real decision there."

"No one knows IT systems more than Kickback." Vanessa turned and pointed to another man who sat at a desk. "I'd like you to meet Scott BeVier. He's from the University of Nebraska on loan to us as part of a political science intern program."

Scott stood and extended his hand.

After shaking, Ava leaned to her sister and lowered her voice. "What did you do, pilfer all Jim's employees?"

Vanessa made an exaggerated shrug. "Not employees...

volunteers. They were free to come and go as they saw fit. I simply lured them with a little monetary incentive. Besides, all is fair in love, war...and politics."

Ava's sister turned to her new team members, not bothering to hide her remarks. "Vanessa Hart only works with the best. These guys are the best. Together, along with all the volunteers we'll recruit, we're going to win this campaign." Her face broke into a wide grin. "Right, guys?"

They both nodded enthusiastically.

"Oh, my goodness, what happened to your hand?" Ava asked after noticing a large red streak across her sister's forearm.

Scott returned to his seat at his desk. "Axel."

"Axel?" Alani asked, confused.

Kickstart lifted from his spot on the floor and brushed off his hands on his jeans. "Jim's mother's cat. Mean as spit, that one."

"Both the mother and the cat," Vanessa added.

Scott laughed. "No worries, though. Vanessa's shoes got the upper hand."

Ava's hand flew to her chest. "Oh, Vanessa. You didn't."

"No...not exactly. These stilettos can kill a small animal. But I did make the horrid thing sorry it messed with me."

Ava couldn't believe what she was hearing. "What did Jim's mother do?"

"Not a lot. I simply held up my shoe in a silent warning not to cross me. She made a wise decision and kept her mouth shut."

Alani appeared shocked. "Better hope no one secretly filmed that exchange on their phone. I can see it now...a viral TikTok video of you clubbing a cat garnering thousands of views."

Vanessa clasped her hands together. "Oh, I wish I'd thought of that."

Kickback grinned and nodded his head. "Yeah...a viral TikTok can pull some serious exposure."

"Of my sister pounding a cat with her high-heeled shoe?" Ava asked with incredulity. "You really think that would win an election?"

Kickback laughed. "Sure. Voters know anyone willing to take on a cat mean as Axel will kick butt in the senate chambers."

"Except, perhaps, all the cat lovers in Hawaii," Alani muttered under her breath.

Hoping to change the subject, Ava pointed to the room's décor. "I like what you've done to the place. It certainly doesn't look like your ordinary campaign office."

The room was expansive and had high ceilings with wooden beams. The walls were freshly painted a light gray which contrasted nicely with the cream leather sofa and overstuffed occasional chairs—the type you might find in a design magazine. There were lots of ceramic pots on the floor filled with plants, and the room smelled like a hotel lobby. "What is that aroma?" Ava asked, sniffing the air.

"It's one of those scent diffusers you find in luxury hotels. Mia secured it for me."

Alani's daughter worked for a mega-resort as a customer relations manager. She'd transferred to the mainland after her affair with Ava's husband had been uncovered and had returned to care for her cancer-ridden mother.

"Well, it's all very...nice. But you haven't officially announced yet. How can you afford all this?"

A sly grin formed on her sister's face. "An in-kind donation from a friend who is a leasing associate for the Shops at Wailea."

Few things out of Vanessa's mouth surprised Ava. But the barely-hidden admission that her sister used her relationships with men for her benefit caused her to simply stare, not knowing what to say.

"Okay, I see the look that just sprouted on your face. I know what I'm doing, Ava." Vanessa spanned her open arms across the room in a Julie Andrews replay from the opening scene in Sound of Music. "Image is everything. Every time the news media gather here for a live interview and my comment on the issues, this office and décor will send the message that this campaign is secure and not struggling for money. We're not functioning on a shoestring. People don't realize it, but subconsciously they like partnering with success. I plan on bringing this campaign to the finish line in a trail of glitter. Every voter in Hawaii will be championing my cause. Why? Because I'm a winner. I know how to influence. Once I land that senate seat, I'll use that influence on their behalf."

Alani leaned close to Ava and shielded her mouth with her hand. "Hmm...a female Trump?"

Ava couldn't help it. She burst out in laughter.

"What's so funny?" Vanessa asked.

"Nothing." Ava tried to maintain a straight face. "Just promise us that you and your supporters will not be wearing red caps and waving closed fists in the air."

5

Christel sat at her dining room table and closed her laptop just as her phone buzzed. She picked it up to an incoming call from her sister.

"Katie, what's up?"

"So, we never got a chance to talk about Aunt Vanessa's announcement."

There it was again, that twinge of jealousy. Politics used to be paramount to her in college. She'd always thought she might dip her toe in, but the reality that her family needed her at Pali Maui took front and center.

"Here's the deal," Katie said. "I think I'm going to head over today and offer to join her staff."

"Her campaign staff?"

"Yeah. What do you think?"

Christel stood and made her way to the fridge, realizing it was mid-afternoon and she hadn't eaten yet. "What does Jon say?"

"I haven't mentioned it yet. No worries. He won't have a problem with it."

"What about Noelle? Surely you don't plan on paying for a

babysitter so you can volunteer?" Christel loved her sister, but she wasn't always financially practical. "And what about the concerts, the gift shop, the tours? Isn't your plate pretty full?"

She could hear her sister sigh with frustration. "None of that demands much of my attention. The gift shop requires me to be there, but only a few hours a day. Willa is now helping out behind the counter after school. She wants to drive, and her dad said she had to earn her own gas money."

Christel foraged for something to eat that didn't require preparation. At the back of the second shelf, she spotted some leftover pizza from two nights ago. While the choice didn't look entirely appetizing, she pulled it out. "That's smart of Jon. Chick-a-dee is at the age where she needs to learn the value of a dollar."

"You're going to make a great mom, Christel."

Her sister's comment stung, reminding her of a long string of failed pregnancy tests. "So, why the campaign?" she said, forcing her mind back to the conversation. "Are you even interested in politics?"

"Of course, I am. I watch CNN and Fox News every night."

Christel put the pizza on a plate and headed for the microwave. "Well...I didn't realize that." She rolled her eyes and pushed the button. "So, who did you vote for in the last presidential election?"

"Oh, I didn't vote. Noelle was still getting up at all hours of the night, and I was too exhausted to go stand in line for hours with her on my hip."

Christel wanted to remind Katie that mail-in ballots and multi-day voting were available. She knew better than to point out these contradictory alternatives to her sister's narrative. Katie would cling to her excuses. "Well, I'm glad you want to get involved now. Good luck."

There was a long pause before Katie cleared her throat and asked, "So, any news?"

The microwave dinged, signaling that the pizza was warm. Christel opened the door and grabbed the plate. "Ouch!"

"What happened?"

"I burned myself." Christel plopped the hot plate on the counter, went for the sink, turned on the cold water, and positioned her injured finger below the stream. "Dang, that hurt."

"You have to be careful," Katie warned.

Christel rolled her eyes a second time. "Thanks, great advice."

"Is someone cranky this morning?"

Christel shut off the water. "No, I simply forgot to eat earlier. I'm hungry."

"Well, hey...I've got a great idea. Why don't you and Evan come over tonight? I'll have Jon leave work early and bring over some amazing food. No need to get dressed up. We'll just hang out, maybe play a game of Catan or something."

"Sorry, sis. Can't. Evan flew out to Honolulu for a medical conference this morning. He's teaching on the fine art of shoulder arthroplasty."

"What's that?"

"I have no clue, but apparently, my husband is an expert in the procedure." Christel returned to the counter and tested the temperature of the pizza. Finding it acceptable, she lifted the slice of pizza to her mouth.

"Evan has been busy a lot lately," Katie noted.

It was true. Her husband had been busier lately. Even when he was home, they seemed to have little to talk about. Their connection had been so focused on getting pregnant, and that had faded with each disappointment. Now, it was as if they'd both carried their hurt and retreated to opposite corners of the room. Christel buried herself in projection and cash flow data while Evan read the latest medical journals and sipped on a glass of his favorite bourbon, despite knowing how nervous nightly drinking made her.

He was mad at her, she knew. Evan wanted her to submit to medical procedures and treatments that might assist their effort to get pregnant. She'd refused. And for good reason. She mentally couldn't bear for her entire world to focus on the goal of creating a child when none of that guaranteed success.

Like Evan, she wanted to be a parent. Personally, she was okay with letting things happen naturally. She'd only agreed to start the process of trying after Evan had shared how much it meant to him.

No pressure there.

"Christel?"

Katie's voice pulled her from her own head. "Yeah. Sorry. I was just thinking about…"

Before she could finish her sentence, Katie interrupted. "Thinking about disappointing Evan."

For someone who, at times, could be as deep as a dime, her sister could also be very astute. Their connection had been forged as kids somewhere between playing Barbies and hanging posters of the Red Hot Chili Peppers on their bedroom walls. She and her sister were as different as night and day. Yet, somehow, Katie knew what she was thinking and how she felt even before she knew herself.

"Yeah. Maybe a little." Christel quietly admitted. "I mean, Evan's being great about everything. I just didn't think it would take this long. Evan wants desperately to be a father. What if I fail him?"

"Oh, honey. You can't think like that. None of this is your fault. Evan knows you want this too."

Christel wanted to embrace that notion. Truly, she did. Yet, in the back of her mind, she couldn't help but wonder. If that were true, why was Evan never home much lately?

6

Aiden crammed the remainder of his hotdog in his mouth and chomped on the nearly cold food while finishing up a monthly report due by the end of the day. He'd been running late all afternoon, ever since the call came in reporting a possible shooter at Kahului Airport. The report was a hoax, fortunately. Still, a potentially explosive situation demanded an all-hands-on-deck response, and every member of his team at the station had dropped what they were doing and went into immediate emergency mode.

Aiden looked over the report data on the screen. He'd just hit the send button when his phone buzzed with an incoming text.

See you soon. ~Shane

Aiden groaned. In the excitement, he'd forgotten about his reluctant promise to meet up with his brother and the mystery guests.

He groaned again. He knew how this would likely go. Shane would set him up with some girl he had nothing in common with and the following hours would be spent trying to find something to talk about. He was too tired to pretend he was having a good time with some woman he was not likely to ever see a second time.

He tossed his used paper plate in the trash and stood.

"Hey."

Aiden turned toward the voice to see Megan standing in the open doorway. "You still here?"

"Uh, isn't that obvious?" She leaned her head against the tiger-tattooed arm stretched against the door jamb. "Someday, huh?"

Aiden nodded. "Can't say I'm sorry things turned out the way they did. Schools and airport shooters...some of my biggest fears."

"You up for grabbing a burger?"

"Sorry, I have plans. Shane thinks my love life sucks, and he's out to fix the sorry fact."

That brought a smile to his co-worker's face. "Ah, one of *those* dates."

Aiden peeled his uniform jacket off and hung it on the designated hook on his office wall. "Yup. Can you see how excited I am?"

"Wow. Yeah, that's some enthusiasm, right there."

They walked out, sprinted down the metal steps together, and then made their way through the nearly empty station. From the smell of spaghetti wafting from the direction of the kitchen, the night crew was catching some dinner.

"Guess I'll head home for a date with Scotch." Megan pulled her long, dark hair back and knotted it at the nape of her neck. "Well, see you tomorrow."

"Yeah. Tomorrow." Aiden gave her a wave and headed for his car.

When Megan first showed up at the station, he had her pegged for a troublemaker, one of those thrill-seekers who took unnecessary risks. Plus, he highly suspected she was out to make a name for herself and replace him.

When he'd been home recovering from the boat accident, she'd been moved into his office, stoking that concern. In the end, his worries were unfounded. He'd been promoted to captain and he had her full support. Especially after he helped extricate her from an abusive relationship.

Megan was one tough chick. She was also extremely beautiful. He couldn't help but wonder why she didn't have a line of guys waiting to take her out and instead was heading home to her dog.

Perhaps, like him, she simply preferred her own company to those who seemed to have rice for brains or were simply looking to hook up.

Aiden hurried home, showered, and pushed the speed limit just a tad in order to be punctual. As soon as he knocked, his brother's door swung open. "You're late," Shane said, waving him inside.

"Sorry. Crazy day at work."

Shane patted him on the back. "Yeah, heard about the airport incident. That's brutal." He led Aiden into the living area where a girl with red hair was sitting on the sofa. "This is Starly Wyatt."

She leaped from the sofa, her cleavage nearly spilling from the low-cut shirt. Her jeans were tight and she wore heels that made her totter while she caught her balance. "Hey, nice to meet you." She extended a hand with long blue-colored nails.

Were those little kittens on them?

Aiden groaned. It was worse than he thought.

Trying to be polite and hide the fact that he wanted to turn and head back out the door, he shook. "Nice to meet you," he muttered.

"Starly works at the Big Wave Taffy shop in Lahaina," Shane offered.

"Yeah, just passed my two-year anniversary. I work Mondays, Wednesdays, and weekends. If I'm lucky, I can pick up some Thursdays when Tonya calls in sick...which is pretty often." She winked. "Kids these days. Don't know responsibility if it bit them in the tush." She giggled at her own wisdom.

Aiden turned his gaze on Shane and gave his younger brother a look that clearly communicated how pleased he was with his date. Never again!

Shane grinned as if reading his mind, then turned as another girl entered the room from down the hall. She was tall and wore a pretty white blouse and blue pants. Very tasteful. Her blonde hair was pulled into a long ponytail.

Aiden couldn't help but stare. She looked like that girl John Kennedy, Jr. married...Carolyn Bessette. He'd always thought she had style.

"This is your date. Aiden, meet Sydney Alexander. She's here visiting her cousin, Starly."

Relief flooded Aiden, followed by a tinge of disappointment to learn the girl was only visiting the island. He immediately reached and shook her hand. "Welcome to Maui. I hope you enjoy your visit."

A timid smile sprouted. "I just got in this morning, but so far, I'm loving everything about Hawaii. You live in such a beautiful place."

"Yeah, sometimes we take it for granted. But there's nothing like these islands...especially Maui. How long are you here?"

"A week. I'm on vacation."

"Oh? Where do you work?" Aiden looked at her intently, wanting to know more about this interesting girl.

"I'm head photographer for a public relations firm in Cincinnati." She raised her eyebrows which were the color of a newborn fawn. "And you?"

Shane motioned for them to have a seat. "Aiden works for Maui Emergency Management Services. He was recently promoted to captain."

"Oh my GOSH! Are you kidding?" Starly asked, her eyes

wide. "That must be so exciting. I mean, just like those shows on television."

Aiden rubbed at the back of his neck. "Well, not exactly."

She drummed her kitten nails on the table, then picked up her can of soda. "So, that's what Shane was talking about...the airport incident. It was all over Twitter. I bet that had the adrenaline pumping. I mean, tell us. What was it like heading into danger like that?"

"There really wasn't any danger," Aiden tried to explain. "It was a hoax."

"Yes, but you didn't know that when you were dispatched. Is that the right word...dispatched?"

Aiden nodded with embarrassment, then glanced at his watch. "What time is our reservation? We don't want to be late."

"We have time," Shane told them. "I let Starly pick the venue for tonight."

His brother's date clapped her blue-kitty-nailed hands together. "We're going to my favorite place for a few beers. The Dirty Monkey." Her eyes filled with more excitement. "They have live music tonight."

The news hit Aiden like a wooden spoon to the head. The Dirty Monkey was their Uncle Jack's hangout. Not exactly a place fitting for a first date with the girl beside him. "Uh, wouldn't you maybe rather catch dinner in Wailea? There's a great seafood place on the beach with a lit pathway perfect for a walk.

"Sounds romantic," Sydney smiled at him.

Yes, he liked this girl.

"No, absolutely not. Sounds far too bougie. Tonight, I'm in the mood to lush up some amber nectar and dance." She giggled again. "Right, Shane?"

He couldn't help but wonder where his brother found this one.

Aiden and Sydney exchanged glances. "Is that okay with

you?" he asked, hoping she might voice some opposition to her cousin's plan. Instead, she gave a weak nod. "Sure...Monkey, whatever it is, is fine."

With their destination settled, they gathered their things and headed outside. "Your car or mine?" Shane asked.

"Mine has gas," Aiden answered.

"Then, yours it is."

Lahaina was less than a half-hour drive from Shane's place in Napili-Honokowai. They pulled up and luckily saw an empty parking spot.

Shane pointed. "There's Uncle Jack's truck."

Aiden looked in that direction. Not far from the front door was a beat-up 1978 Chevy Silverado.

"Your Uncle Jack?" Sydney asked.

"Yeah. Our mom's brother, aka Captain Jack, as he's known to locals. He owns the Cane Fire, a hard-bottom inflatable that launches here out of Lahaina. He ferries tourists over to Lanai for snorkeling and whale-watching excursions."

"Really? I'd love to do that," Sydney said as Aiden helped her from the car.

Aiden jumped on the opening. "Perhaps I can take you while you're here."

She smiled back at him. "I'd like that."

"C'mon, let's go!" Starly urged. "Sounds like the music has already started."

Inside, the lighting was dim. Several seconds passed before Aiden's eyes adjusted and he could make out the crowded bar and tables. There was a stage located against the rear wall that was really a makeshift platform made of wooden pallets. Three guys sat on stools, two with guitars and one parked behind a very loud set of drums.

Uncle Jack noticed them right off and waved them over. "Well, look who the cats drug in." He leaned and said something to a couple of guys sitting at the bar next to him. They nodded and got up.

"Don't leave on our account," Shane said.

"Nah, these are my guys. They've got a boat to clean. I just was oiling 'em up first." He let out a raucous laugh and rubbed his generous belly which protruded from an open Hawaiian-print shirt. "Sit, sit." He waved the bartender over, a native who wore thick eyeglasses and was balding on top. "Noa, let's set these fine folks up." Jack looked over them. "Anything you want. On me. And, keep them coming."

Shane ordered a beer. So did Starly. Aiden couldn't remember if the Dirty Monkey served craft beers. When he asked, his voice got drowned out by the start of another song. He gave up. "I'll just have whatever's on draft," he shouted.

He turned to Sydney, leaning in close in order to be heard. "Do you want beer, or perhaps a glass of wine?"

His date shook her head. "Henry McKenna single barrel."

His eyes shot up in surprise. "Scotch?"

She nodded and hollered across the bar to the bartender. "A double, please."

With their drinks in hand, they parked on the bar stools emptied by Uncle Jack's guys. Aiden hated that it was so noisy. How could he possibly hold a conversation with this girl? He wanted to get to know her, even if her stay might be short. It wasn't often he met up with someone who was beautiful, and intelligent. He wanted to know everything about her.

After several attempts at conversation met with Sydney cupping her hand around her ear and saying, "Huh? What?" he finally gave up. He politely pointed to her nearly empty glass. "Another?"

He was surprised when she nodded enthusiastically. "Sure. Another double."

Over the next hour, he was even more surprised when she waved over the bartender several more times. "Another, please."

By the third time, her words had slowed. By the fourth order, her head bobbed slightly and she struggled to pronounce the words without slurring.

Aiden frowned with concern. "You okay?" he asked, now worried about her inebriated state. He rarely saw men four times the size of her slight frame able to ingest that much alcohol and still walk.

She grabbed his hand. "Let's dance!" She pointed to the tight space in front of the stage where Shane and Starly had already migrated.

Aiden wasn't fond of dancing, and less so in such a crowded place where any movement invited bumping into another individual. Shane looked to be having a good time and Starly tossed her head back, laughing.

Despite the frenetic beat of the music, Sydney stepped next to him, plopped her head against his chest, and flopped her limp arms over his shoulders. She rocked back and forth, slowly singing the lyrics from *Shallow* by Lady Gaga. At least he thought that's what she was singing.

He looked down and noticed she only wore one shoe.

Aiden closed his eyes and groaned. Sydney's head suddenly popped up and she tore at the front of her blouse, popping a button. It flew to the floor and bounced away under the feet of the crowd. "It's hot in here," she said, her words thick, but now completely clear. She glanced around. "I need a drink."

"I'm not sure that's a good..." His voice drifted as she pulled away and pushed through the dancers in the direction of the bar. He had no choice but to follow.

Halfway to her destination, she halted and turned to face him. Her eyes were wild and frantic.

"What's the matter?" he asked, quickly closing the space between them. Sydney's actions tonight were nothing in line with what he'd expected from a girl who had appeared to be so cultured.

His date didn't answer. Instead, her chin flopped to her chest. She lifted her head just in time to mutter, "I—I think I'm going to be sick."

Before Aiden could react, she opened her mouth and spewed vomit across the floor at his feet. Chunks bounced off his open sandals.

He closed his eyes and released a long moan.

This.

This was why he didn't date.

7

Vanessa Hart didn't do anything in a small way, especially when it came to promoting herself.

She couldn't help but smile at the proof of that sentiment as she looked around the grand ballroom at the Four Seasons in Wailea. The venue had been pricey, for sure. But worth every penny.

It was here that she was going to formally announce her candidacy. All the stops had been pulled out for potential supporters, donors, and the media. Vanessa needed to come across as a winner right from the start. She'd spared no cost to do so.

Thankfully, her early fundraising efforts had garnered enough contributions to cover this splash. Her budget would be cut in other ways, in manners not seen in the public eye.

Katie, her new campaign manager, approached wielding a clipboard and a pen. "Countdown to lift off," she announced, gleaming.

Her niece had no campaign experience to speak of, but she was willing to donate her time on a volunteer basis. Vanessa would be the one running the show anyway. Katie would provide much-needed backup, do her bidding, and learn along the way.

"Great job," Vanessa told her. She twirled with outstretched arms. "How do I look?"

"That skirt and jacket definitely scream power suit." Katie looked around, surveying the activity in the room. "I'm surprised Christel approved the line-item expense," she said, teasing. "My sister can be a real pain in the butt when it comes to spending money."

After much coercing, Christel had agreed to serve as campaign treasurer, again with no remuneration. They would no doubt butt heads over matters, but Vanessa trusted her. More than one campaign had run ashore because the money ran out. Christel would keep that from happening.

Katie spotted two hotel staff electricians gathering their things. She waved them over. "Make sure we have proper wattage to the speakers. I want everyone to be able to hear when the candidate makes her announcement. And don't forget to test the microphones." Katie turned from the electricians to the men crossing the room toting large baskets of miniature pink azaleas and white dendrobium orchids. "Thanks, guys. Let's place those so that they line the stage at the front of the ballroom."

Her cell phone broke through the noisy preparations. "Katie here."

With her head pressed to her tiny phone, she waved at a girl carrying a rack of stemware and pointed her to the other side of the room. The girl pivoted and headed that way. Katie returned her attention to the phone call. "Thanks, Ben. You're the best."

Satisfied, she pocketed her phone and tucked the clipboard under her arm. "Okay, we're ready to go," she announced, then scurried off toward the kitchen.

Ava arrived with her hand looped in Tom Strobe's arm. Her sister always looked lovely but even more so now that she was in love. Tom was a catch, and Ava adored the man who had renovated her golf course—and her broken heart.

Vanessa waved and moved to greet them. "So, what do you think?"

Ava looked all around. "Nice. Quite the production. A lot of work, I imagine."

That was an understatement. "You don't even know the half of it. Luckily, we have many people who volunteered to help out, including your wonderful daughters."

Ava nodded. "You don't have to tell me how amazing they are. I very much admire the women they've become."

Ava gave her a pointed look. "You have a great daughter, too, you know."

Vanessa opened her mouth to argue, but the look on her sister's face stopped her. "Well, that supposition could be debated. I mean, I haven't seen her in over a year."

After an extended and very nasty divorce, Vanessa's daughter had chosen to live with her father. Attempts made to reach out were all rebuffed. The fact was, like any sixteen-year-old girl who was spoiled rotten by a man using her as a weapon in a divorce war, Isabelle had an attitude. One Vanessa prayed she would grow out of when she finally realized her mother wasn't the monster her father made her out to be.

Ava reached for her arm. "You should call her. You don't want her learning you are running for senator from the news."

Vanessa sighed. Her sister was right. No doubt, the stations in the Seattle area would jump on the opportunity to exploit a story about their disgraced former news anchor turned candidate. There was only one major problem. Isabelle rarely picked up the phone or responded to her texts, no matter how often she reached out. Given that, Vanessa figured it was better not to poke the bear and wait for her to make her way out of hibernation, even if it took a year or so.

She'd be here, waiting.

As the next hours passed, the room filled. Overhead, massive chandeliers cast light over linen-draped tables lined with chairs. White floral centerpieces decorated the center of the tables. Specially invited industry guests from all the islands were in attendance, as well as locals. A bank of media cameras lined the back of the room.

When it was time, a hired announcer wearing a tuxedo took the dais at the front of the ballroom and introduced himself as the director of the Friends of Hawaii, a non-profit that served the state's interests by championing important causes and those candidates the organization deemed worthy of support. It had been a real coup for Vanessa to bring them to her side by promising that, if elected, she would direct state budget dollars in their favor. "Good evening, everyone. Thank you for coming out tonight for this little party."

A roar of applause swept through the audience.

While he continued talking, Vanessa smiled and nodded to a staffer, then patted the back of the hotel security guard.

"And now, without further ado...let's bring up the woman of the hour, the one who, with all our help, will be our next state senator!"

Vanessa climbed the steps up to the dais, waving to the crowd. She wore a bright red suit with matching heels and her hair tucked into a precise bun at the nape of her neck. She smiled widely, then held up an open palm, quieting another round of applause. She stepped up to the mic.

"Hello, Maui!"

In a carefully calculated interruption, the band at the back of the room started playing what would become her campaign theme song, a tune made famous by Adele. With permission, the lyrics were altered, and everyone joined in belting out, "There's a fire burning deep in Vanessa Hart, our next senator who will bring us out of the dark." The crowd gleefully joined in belting out the following line. "And we can have it all."

The song was Katie's idea, a brilliant choice. Vanessa was already seeing how that girl held promise.

Vanessa couldn't help but get swept up in the passion. For maybe the first time, she considered that she really could upend Jim Kahale's bid and become senator.

"Thank you, everyone," she said as the music finally wound down. "I appreciate you all being with me today as we formally announce my candidacy for senator from Maui!"

The crowd erupted again, prompted by planted supporters, including her brother Jack, who wore cream-colored linen slacks and a matching Hawaiian print shirt completely buttoned for the occasion.

Over the next twenty minutes, Vanessa shared her vision... one she'd initially crafted for Jim Kahele but had now spun to sound like her own. The message was delivered with a sense of passion Jim lacked and a purpose that seemed to hit the heart of the assembled crowd and had them fired up.

"This campaign is about serving the people of Maui, making sure your concerns are addressed in the state capitol building in Honolulu. And, with all your help, we'll get this done. We'll change the landscape of what is ahead for our great state. Together, we'll make a difference! Together, we'll win!"

The crowd immediately went to their feet, and applause roared across the ballroom. Behind the dais, red, white, and blue balloons were released. Red and blue smoke rose from pillars secured behind the stage. Her theme song started up again.

Vanessa was beside herself with glee. Why hadn't she considered politics earlier? She was born for this.

As she finally moved to step down from the dais, Katie

thrust her cell phone into her hands. "Aunt Vanessa, your phone has been buzzing and buzzing. Caller unknown."

Vanessa immediately determined to brush off the annoyance until her phone buzzed again. This time, her ex-husband's name appeared, followed by a single-line text.

Isabelle has been arrested.

8

Vanessa's heart missed a beat. "What do you mean arrested?"

"Our daughter was caught protesting climate change, and a boardwalk down on the wharf was set ablaze," her ex-husband reported.

Oh, now he claimed Isabelle was *their* daughter and not his exclusively. "And they arrested her?"

"Street camera video shows a crowd of young people. It isn't clear who exactly lit the match and tossed it into the spilled gasoline. And none of them are talking."

In the background, Vanessa could hear the noise from her big party. She shielded the phone from view and tersely whispered, "I can't deal with this now. In case you hadn't heard, I just announced my candidacy for senate...like ten minutes ago." She swallowed the massive lump in her throat, trying to push images of the tiny little girl who used to lay her head against her shoulder out of her mind. "I'll call you the minute I'm able to talk."

"Oh, here we go again. Too busy."

"Clark, stop. I said I'd call you." She tried to shake off the building anger forming in her gut. She had a lot to say, the least of which was to dish up a hefty dose of criticism. His parenting skills were to blame here, not hers. "Unless you want me to talk about this sensitive issue in front of the media."

"Oh, no...let's not have that." His voice grew bitter. "We all know how nasty the media can be."

That was it...the thing that put her over. Vanessa huffed and hung up on him.

"Aunt Vanessa? Is everything okay?" Katie looked at her with worry.

"Not exactly, but I'll deal with it." She drew a deep breath and pasted the brightest smile she could muster before she moved back into the room and her adoring supporters... backers who all wanted something from her and expected her to deliver.

The Lodging and Tourism council bent her ear for nearly twenty minutes, making sure she understood their concerns over the passage of a potential hotel moratorium. The president of the organization held up his nearly-empty glass of bourbon. "We'd like to extend our endorsement and make it official, but first, we need to get you on the record that you would help defeat this endeavor."

Vanessa placed a perfectly manicured hand on his forearm. "I promise you won't have to wonder where I stand on the issue. Tourism is essential to the health and welfare of this island. While I am not prepared to make a formal statement at this juncture regarding how I plan to deal with the moratorium, I assure you that every one of your members will have their pens ready to sign their support for me when I do." She winked.

A gaggle of teachers gathered around her to voice their concerns about the lack of state-funded after-school programs. "We will not let our youth down," she promised. "It comes down to a matter of budget. The solution is to meticulously scrutinize our current spending and find the funds."

A short woman who sported a unibrow and a severe frown stepped forward and argued. "Budget is what politicians always hide behind."

Vanessa's rebuttal was polite but firm. "No matter our desires, metaphorically speaking, we don't pay the electric company, and they turn our lights off. The leaders in our state can't approach this critical issue willy-nilly. We must look to the future and ensure that whatever decision is made on behalf of our children cannot be overturned for lack of funds next fiscal year or the next. Monetary prudence is essential here." She smiled at the woman along with the others. "Even so, as your senator, I vow to do everything in my power to extend this much-needed service to our communities."

She said this, knowing that a reporter from the local news station had wandered close and was standing behind her. She turned and smiled at him. "Hello, I don't believe we've met."

The guy was tall and lanky with shoulder-length hair the color of peanut butter. In contrast, his eyes were dark blue... broody and piercing. "I have a question," he said. "On the record."

Vanessa enticed him with a smile. "Sure, go ahead." She knew his type, and rarely could a media bulldog get the best of her.

He introduced himself as Jeff Markum and waved over his camera crew. With a microphone extended, he tucked his chin and glanced at his notes. When he raised his head, he looked her directly in the eyes.

"Would you care to comment on the recent arrest of your minor daughter for arson?"

9

Vanessa would have kept the incident with Isabelle a secret, but for the headlines she knew would show up in the morning. Given that weasel reporter's investigative skills, she'd been forced to come clean.

"Arrested?" Ava's hand flew to her chest. "Oh, no. That's awful."

Christel voiced a similar sentiment. "Oh, goodness. I hate hearing that."

Katie parked her hands on her hips. "What was she thinking? Does she know how her choices impact this campaign?"

Ava rubbed her younger daughter's back. "I'm not certain she knew her mother was running."

The information caused Katie's eyes to widen. "Oh."

Vanessa's insides were trembling. Still, she couldn't let on. "Look, I'm sure this isn't what it initially appears. I've already booked a redeye out tonight and will be in Seattle by morning. I'll get all this sorted out." She glanced around at her family. "Until then, this campaign moves forward. We have a lot of work ahead of us. This is a minor blip. Believe me when I tell you that news cycles are short. This may be sexy news right now, but the impact will wear off quickly. People will bore and move on."

Ava scowled. "But, what about Isabelle?"

Vanessa carefully hid her emotions from her sister. Any crack, and she'd break. She hadn't survived Clark abandoning her, losing her job and her daughter, and being financially destitute by going soft when things got hard.

"As I told you, I'll be there by morning and will deal with Isabelle," she explained with emphasis. End of the discussion.

Ava opened her mouth, then paused as if she had reconsidered what she was about to say.

The overnight flight took just under six hours. Her plane landed at Sea-Tac and taxied to the terminal just as the dove gray sky dawned over the horizon. Vanessa hadn't bothered to pack a suitcase. She didn't plan to be here long and an overnight bag would do.

Outside the terminal, she waved down a taxi and ducked several large raindrops as she scrambled into the passenger seat. She gave the driver the address to her hotel, then leaned her head back, hoping to rest her eyes for a few minutes.

A loud honk immediately thwarted her plan. The taxi driver yelled at the car in front of him and shook his fist.

Vanessa gave up and stared out the window at the dismal scenery.

Contrary to popular belief, the sun does occasionally appear in Seattle. When it's not raining, people who live in the Pacific Northwest have been known to drop everything and rush to their favorite outdoor spot—head out on a hike, take a dip in a local lake, pack a picnic and find a grassy spot—it's all part of embracing the wonderful weather.

Those days were few and far between. Most were like the sky above, drizzly and chilly.

Vanessa was tempted to take a nap before heading to her ex-husband's place, but she knew better than to try. She hadn't slept all night, unable to keep thoughts of Isabelle at bay.

A protest? Perhaps. But, arrested for starting a fire? Destruction of public property? That was not her daughter. No matter their estrangement, she knew Isabelle and those actions were out of character. She most certainly did not believe her daughter to be the one who actually set the fire. Legal counsel would make sure that was clear if it came to that.

Her daughter resembled Ava. She believed rules were to be followed. There were appropriate ways to influence change without crossing established social boundaries.

Anger rose inside.

Clark had been derelict in his parental duties...that's all there was to it. How often had he made the point that he was there for Isabelle when Vanessa wasn't? She'd run smack dab into a wall of criticism for every missed play, every occasion where she'd had to drop everything and fly somewhere for the next big story instead of standing at a hot stove and cooking dinner for the family, every time she'd shown up late to a school meeting.

He had little regard for how difficult things were for her at the station, at the intense competition, and how many young, beautiful girls were in the wings waiting for their opportunity in front of the camera...the ones willing to extend all kinds of favors for the chance to unseat her as lead anchor.

Clark was a real estate investor. His success seemed far more important than her career, even though her former husband had enjoyed more than a few favors extended because she might be of use to his business associates. Good press was worth its weight in gold, especially to developers vying for permits and favorable zoning decisions.

Well, Isabelle's arrest had happened on his watch. There would be no arguing that fact. She could hardly wait to face him and tell him so.

By eight o'clock a.m., Vanessa was standing on Clark's doorstep with her finger on the doorbell.

When the door opened, her ex stood there looking like he had slept in his clothes. His precise haircut was unkempt and his face held the color of uncooked chicken.

"Well, you look good," Vanessa said, not bothering to hide the snark in her voice.

"Vanessa." He leaned and brushed an obligatory kiss against her cheek.

"Well, where is she?" she demanded. "I want to talk to her."

He reached and placed his hand on her arm, gave her a weak smile. "She's asleep. I think we need to talk first."

Vanessa shrugged off his attempt at reconciliation. "*We* have nothing to say."

That's when she heard a noise. Across the room, a woman lifted from the sofa wearing a white button-down shirt tucked inside a pair of tan slacks. Her neck-length dark brown hair was pushed behind one ear and stylish tortoise-shell glasses were parked on her petite nose.

"Who is this?" Vanessa barked, not bothering to use any manners.

Clark rubbed his hand across his head, causing even more havoc with his hair. "This is Julie. My wife."

IN RETROSPECT, Vanessa might have been more kind.

The news caught her off guard. She hated feeling blindsided.

Despite her replacement's attempt at being gracious, Vanessa donned full-witch mode. "Well, nice of you to alert me to the fact you'd remarried. Geez, Clark. I see you still can't see past your own face." Feeling especially mean, Vanessa turned to the woman, who was now slowly removing her glasses. "I hope you know what you signed up for. Do you cook? Clean? I hope you know how to host the perfect dinner party. Oh, and iron. Clark will want all the dinner napkins perfectly pressed. Do you have a career of your own?" She released an ugly laugh. "Better say goodbye to that." She pointed back at Clark with her thumb. "'Ole Mr. Entitled won't like that one bit."

Clark grabbed her wrist. "Vanessa, that's enough."

Tears threatened. She bit the inside of her cheek to keep from letting them appear. Instead, she laughed. "Lighten up, Clark," she said, pulling away. "You don't think I care that you hooked one of your many women into marrying you, do you? Or that you didn't tell me?"

She turned to Julie. "I mean, why would I care?"

Julie coughed and let her gaze drift to the hallway.

Vanessa followed her gaze with her own.

"Stop!" Isabelle screamed. "Just stop fighting."

Vanessa had trouble breathing.

Her daughter, whom she hadn't seen in over a year, was beautiful.

Even in her anger and tears, the young girl—now almost a woman—was the most stunning creature Vanessa had laid her eyes on.

Immediately, nothing else matters. She desperately wanted to go to her, fold her frame against her body, and hug her tight. Sadly, she had forfeited the privilege with her outburst. When it came to Isabelle, it seemed she could never do anything right.

All eyes were on her. She only had moments to decide what came next.

10

Ava headed out her front door to join Christel, who opened her trunk and bent inside to retrieve a flat of canna lily starts. Earlier, her daughter had called to report that a new color had arrived at their favorite nursery, a pretty coral shade with specs of yellow.

Ava peered inside the trunk for a closer look. "Those are gorgeous. And there's plenty enough to share with Alani."

Christel nodded with a smile. "Yes, Alani loves her flowers. I was told this color is scarce."

"Do you want to drive over with me to deliver them?" she asked, hopefully.

Christel shook her head. "Nah, just tell her I love her, and I'm tickled to hear the good news."

Ava's best friend had suffered a battle with breast cancer. With aggressive and early treatment, the dreadful disease retreated.

"Yes, prayers were answered. It looks like the worst is behind her. No more rounds of radiation or chemo. No more fatigue and days spent huddled over the toilet." Ava couldn't help it. She teared up. "I'm not sure I would have survived losing her."

Christel pulled her mother into an encouraging hug. "But, you didn't."

Embarrassed at her sudden emotion, Ava wiped at the moisture in her eyes. "No." She turned to face her daughter square on. "But, listen. You can't keep avoiding Mia. She's back, and there will be times you'll run into her on the island. Don't you think it's time you found a way to put the anger aside? I'm not asking you to be best friends. Goodness knows I will never view her the same after what she did to our family." She reached for her daughter's arm as she lifted the flat of plants from the trunk. "For your sake, baby...get past this and find a way not to let her actions haunt you. Your father wouldn't want that. Neither do I."

"My father lost the right to have a say in the matter...in any part of my life," she responded bitterly. "The two of them crossed a sacred line. I'm glad you can forgive them both, Mom. I can't."

Ava saw the truth in what her daughter claimed, yet she believed with all her heart that people were robbed of the power to hurt you when you took your life back and forgave. Lincoln and Mia had each paid for their indiscretions in multiple ways. Lincoln paid the ultimate price by losing his life in an accident on the way back from a clandestine meeting with his lover. Mia exchanged love and respect for shame and self-loathing.

No matter the forgiveness, or even the repentant heart...bad choices still had consequences.

Ava changed the subject as she followed her daughter through the gate and around to the lanai overlooking the pool. "How is Evan? I haven't seen him in what seems like ages."

"Yeah, I haven't seen him in ages either," Christel muttered.

Before Ava could follow up on the comment, a familiar voice rang out. "Hey, you two."

Christel and Ava turned to see Katie walking toward them from the direction of her house.

"Are you having a party and leaving me out?" Katie marched through the gate and joined them, carrying a box of croissants. "I dropped Noelle off at nursery school and couldn't help myself. They're from that new bakery just blocks from her school."

Ava waved her over. "Welcome to the party, darling."

"Yeah, you say that only because you're hungry," Katie teased.

Christel placed the flat of plants on the ground and brushed off her hands on the front of her pants. "Let me go inside and wash. You two want anything?"

"I left an iced coffee on the counter. Be a dear and bring it to me?" Ava asked.

"You want something, Katie?" Christel waited. "By the way, what are you even doing here? I thought you'd be over at the campaign office."

"I'm heading there after we have our treat," Katie told them. "Right now, so many things are on hold until Aunt Vanessa returns from Seattle."

Ava lifted a croissant from the box. "I thought my sister was only going to be gone overnight."

Katie pointed. "By the way, there's a container of honey butter." She plopped into a nearby patio chair. "From what I gather, Aunt Vanessa ran into a little trouble."

Ava spread some honey butter on her croissant. "Trouble?"

Katie nodded. "Yup. Apparently, dealing with the Isabelle issue hasn't been as easy as expected. Her daughter got in some trouble and was arrested."

11

"What do you mean, you want Isabelle to come live with me?"

"Calm down, Vanessa. We talked and believe it's best for everyone if..."

"Oh, don't give me that crap, Clark. I'm sure by everyone you mean you and the new Mrs. Masters. A difficult daughter is hell on a new marriage, right?" Vanessa's fists clenched by her side. "I mean, first you selfishly grab our daughter away from me to make a point, and now you're giving her back because she's too much trouble? You are a classic jerk, Clark. All the way around."

"Ssh...keep your voice down," he warned, his face looking tired and distraught.

"Or, what?" Vanessa countered. "She's not a dog, Clark. You can't just return her to the pound."

"You're one to talk. You left her there in the first place."

Vanessa's blood reached the boiling point. "You have a nice way of rewriting the story. Let me recount the way it all went down. Chapter one, I was strolling down Pike Place Market, Starbucks in hand, when what do I see? My husband with his nose nuzzled against some blonde's neck. Chapter two? A little research and I find hotel charges in our bank account...hotels located right here in town. Chapter three? I confront the dirty dog and he says it's my fault! MY fault!"

Clark rubbed the bridge of his nose. "There's no benefit in rehashing all this."

"No? Chapter four, I'm told it was my career that ended us. I was away from home too much. I didn't keep up the laundry, the cooking, the cleaning." Her eyes grew cold as steel. "That I wasn't a good mother."

"You left me," he reminded.

She jabbed her finger in his direction, not bothering to hide her bitterness. "What choice did you give me?"

Vanessa tried to calm herself. Nothing would be gained by losing control. "I am happy to take my daughter." She leaned forward. "It's obvious you've lost control and failed her."

Clark stood. "Maybe this isn't a good idea after all. Like you said, you are in the middle of a highly public campaign. I'm not sure you'll have the time needed to help guide her back to herself."

"Yes, I'm sure being tossed aside by her father while he chases another skirt has messed her up."

"I am married, Vanessa. This isn't a fling. We love each other and just need some time to focus on us for a while."

"Oh, that is royal." Vanessa couldn't believe what she was hearing. She held up open palms. "Look, you don't have to argue and convince me. I've known for a long time you would eventually let Isabelle down and I'd have to pick up the pieces of the wreckage."

"This, coming from the Drama Queen."

Ugh! She wanted to punch that smug look right off his face. The truth was he'd tossed both of them aside for another woman, just at separate times.

As good as it felt to let him have it, this verbal jousting was getting her nowhere. The lenient Seattle judge had given them all a break by granting a dismissal after another girl admitted to lighting the fire. That was followed by a stern warning. "You only have one life, young lady. I hope you choose more wisely in the future."

Vanessa didn't need a war with Clark. What she needed was to gather her daughter and return to Maui. She had the campaign to get back to...and now, a relationship to repair.

Some would argue the fact that mending her fractured relationship with Isabelle mattered to her, especially her ex-husband and even her sister Ava, who could lean against the judgment pole at times. From the time she was a little girl and lost her own mother, she learned how to hide her hurt and pretend she was much stronger inside than she really was.

The truth?

She loved her daughter. From the time she was born, she worried constantly about whether to breast or bottle feed, if the cream she was using to treat her daughter's diaper rash was filled with chemicals that would be harmful when absorbed into newborn skin, and whether her little girl's cries were hungry cries or simply a sign she was growing sleepy. Babies didn't come with manuals.

Back then, to look down at her tiny, up-turned nose, to hold her in her arms, was to say a final farewell to her own heart. There was no way to know at the time how deeply Isabelle would shatter her mother's heart, or how easily Vanessa could break hers.

Yes, she'd thrown everything into her career. Focusing on the news station kept her from having to face the fact that her husband had been unfaithful. Something she'd never disclosed to anyone, not even Ava, when her sister faced the same.

Isabelle believed the lies and garbage fed to her by her dad. In the aftermath of the divorce, she chose to live with Clark. Despite the mask Vanessa constantly wore to hide the fact, leaving without her daughter had sliced her to the core and left her bleeding.

Finally, she'd been given the opportunity for a fresh start with her daughter.

She wasn't going to mess it up this time.

12

Vanessa tucked the boarding passes inside her wallet after they cleared security. "You want to grab something at the Starbucks kiosk before we head to our gate?"

Isabelle deepened her scowl. "Sure. Whatever."

Vanessa ignored her daughter's surly response and smiled. "Okay, then...let's head that way."

The air terminal was crowded and noisy. They jumped to avoid a family running as if they were going to miss their flight. The harried mom held a toddler's hand, nearly dragging the poor kid behind her. Close behind, the dad maneuvered the stroller and kept shouting for her to hurry.

They reached the coffee line to find a long string of people winding for what seemed like forever. Given the expected wait, Vanessa would've chosen to skip getting coffee altogether, but she needed the boost the caffeine would provide. Especially after the late night she'd had listening to Isabelle and her father in the other room shout and argue when he'd broken the news to her.

It was unlikely that Isabelle had gotten much sleep either.

Her daughter was angry. Every expression, every glance, and every word from her girl's mouth conveyed that she was the target of Isabelle's blame.

For the next thirty minutes, Vanessa stood in line with Isabelle, who had her face buried in her phone. When it was finally their turn to order, Vanessa turned to her daughter. "What do you want, honey?"

"Nothing."

"Nothing? Are you sure?"

Isabelle looked at her like she didn't have the sense of a grasshopper. Her sullen daughter didn't bother to respond a second time; she simply looked down at her phone again.

Vanessa drew a deep breath and turned to the young kid behind the counter. "I'll have a package of egg bites, a large dark-roast Americano, and a blended Caramel Ribbon Crunch."

"Size?"

"Vente," she told him, pulling her credit card from her wallet. She countered the look she got from Isabelle with, "You might change your mind."

Her daughter shrugged. "Not likely."

The flight from Seattle to Maui was nearly seven hours. Seven long hours of what was primarily silence sprinkled with a few grunts and a lot of sighs. Vanessa made attempts at conversation. Each time her efforts were met with cold and apathetic shrugs. Finally, she gave up and focused on editing her upcoming speech for an event at the tourism council.

"Ladies and gentlemen, Hawaiian Airlines welcomes you to Kahului Airport. The local time in Maui is four o'clock. For your safety and the safety of those around you, please remain seated with your seat belt fastened and keep the aisle clear until we are parked at the gate."

Vanessa closed her laptop and slid it back into her bag. She looked over at Isabelle, who made no attempt to follow the announced instructions. "Honey, your tray," Vanessa urged. "You need to put it up."

Isabelle ignored her.

Vanessa gave her a gentle nudge with her shoulder. "Did you hear me?"

Again, nothing.

Vanessa's jaw set. She loved this girl, but she was not putting up with her insolence. Respect had to be established immediately. Affection could follow later.

She took a deep breath and placed her hand over her daughter's. She squeezed slightly. "Put up the tray." There was no missing her meaning.

Isabelle narrowed her eyes, slammed the tray up, and clicked the hook.

"Thank you," Vanessa said.

At the baggage claim, Vanessa attempted to lighten the mood. "So, I can take you shopping before you start classes if you want. There are some amazing shops in Wailea."

"Don't worry about it. I have my own credit card."

"What?"

"Dad gave me a credit card. I don't have to depend on you." She nearly sneered. "Thanks, though."

Vanessa took a deep breath, pulled her mental shield in place, and fired off what she knew would start a battle. She held out an open palm. "I'll need you to give that to me."

Isabelle's eyes grew wide. "No way. It's mine."

"If you need anything, I'll pay for it. The card." She left her open palm extended. When Isabelle failed to comply, she said, "Now."

Isabelle's face flushed with anger. "Sure. Dad told me you were a control freak." She made a big show of digging in her wallet and removing the card. She slapped it into her mother's hand. "There. Happy?"

That's when she saw Jim Kahale's mother standing in the

crowd of people on the other side of the claim station. She had her cat in her arms and stared without compunction.

Vanessa wanted to stick her tongue out at the sour-faced woman and her miserable feline. Instead, she forced herself to look away just in time before her designer luggage passed out of reach on the chugging metal conveyor. She bent and lifted the bag and settled it at her feet.

"I couldn't be happier," she told Isabelle.

13

Isabelle had seven large suitcases, which accrued an extra baggage fee Vanessa didn't even want to think about. All but one bag came out on the turn style. Isabelle looked panicked.

"But, that's the one with all my shoes," she moaned.

Vanessa slipped her hand onto her daughter's shoulder. "It'll get here. Sometimes a bag will be left behind, temporarily. When discovered, the attendants ensure the missing piece is sent on the next flight. Come on, let's go talk to someone and make a report." She said this while calculating how they would get all these bags into her car.

She grabbed the handle of the baggage cart when a flash of color caught her eye. She looked to see balloons in the air held by the hands of her family members who were standing just outside the glass doors.

"Surprise!" they shouted in unison as she and Isabelle exited the baggage claim area.

There was her sister, Ava. Christel was there, smiling. Katie and her entire family stood nearby. Little Noelle pointed overhead. "Badoon, badoon."

Aiden waved while Shane juggled little Carson on his hip.

Vanessa grinned. The welcoming committee was here to greet Isabelle. She glanced over and was happy to see a tiny smile on her daughter's face. "Look, sweetheart. They all came to welcome you."

The following minutes were filled with hugs, kisses, and lots of chatter. Everyone was happy that Isabelle was here on the island. No one mentioned her recent indiscretion or questioned the events that prefaced her arrival. They simply made Isabelle feel welcome.

"Here, let me help with the bags," Aiden offered.

She smiled at her nephew, grateful for the assistance. Shane passed off Carson into Isabelle's arms. "I'll help."

"Me, too," Jon said.

Isabelle's face lit up as she gazed into the tiny guy's face. She placed her nose against his. "Well, hello, sweet guy. How are you?"

He answered by grabbing a fistful of her hair and bringing it to his mouth.

She laughed and extricated the strands from his grip. "Not sure that will taste good."

Ava placed her arm around Isabelle's shoulder. "We are so delighted you are here, Isabelle. I can't wait to show you around Pali Maui."

Katie chimed in. "You're going to love the island, Isabelle."

"I hope you're up for some surfing," Aiden told her, heaving two suitcases in each hand.

They all headed for the tram that would take them to the parking garage.

Vanessa smiled. Families were messy, but she had a good one. First, they'd given her a home and the support she'd needed when she found herself down and out after being fired from the news station. Now, they were opening their arms to her wayward daughter.

She leaned to her sister and lowered her voice. "Thank you."

Ava smiled back at her. "It's the least we could do. She's family."

That evening, they spent time at Ava's. Despite all the work ahead of them to get Isabelle settled, Vanessa was grateful she didn't have to maneuver those first hours staring at her daughter, who stared at her phone.

After Ava and Katie took Isabelle for a quick look around Pali Mali, they all gathered on the lanai for a quick dinner. Vanessa was amused to see the glint in her daughter's eyes as she focused on the beautiful pool.

Ava noticed as well. "You can come over and swim anytime you wish, honey." She pulled Isabelle into a brief shoulder hug. "I hope you're hungry."

Jon grilled hamburgers and hotdogs; both garnished with a relish of roasted pineapple, onion, and ground macadamia nuts. Katie made them all blended drinks made with pineapple, guava juice, and ice cream. She adorned the glasses with maraschino cherries and tiny paper umbrellas.

After filling their stomachs, they headed inside and played charades. Isabelle laughed when Aiden acted out the film Pretty Woman by swaying his hips back and forth and fluttering his eyelashes. When it was Vanessa's turn, she stood and held up four fingers.

"What category?" Christel asked.

"Oh, sorry." Vanessa kicked off her stilettos, a signal she was about to get serious. "Book title."

She held up one finger to designate the first word. When she was sure everyone understood, she motioned that the word was short and held up two fingers.

"Wait. Are we guessing the first word still? Or, the second?" Ava asked.

Vanessa shook her head and held up two fingers.

"Two!" Shane shouted.

Vanessa nodded enthusiastically.

"How'd you get that?" Katie shook her head. "I was with Mom. I couldn't even tell which word Aunt Vanessa was going for."

Vanessa didn't let the criticism sway her effort. She held up two fingers.

Katie let out a heavy sigh. "Second word...at least I hope it is."

Vanessa confirmed with a nod. She grabbed an imaginary person and made wild stabbing motions.

Shane rolled his eyes. "Too easy. Kill." He reached for Isabelle's lap and clucked his little son's chin. "To Kill a Mockingbird."

"Yes!" Vanessa clapped her hands with glee. "You got it." Did anyone really think they could beat someone like her who made her living communicating?

The game continued, each of them taking turns. Despite a heroic effort, no one guessed mowing a lawn, Elsa from the Disney movie Frozen, or baking cookies. Finally, Vanessa glanced at her watch. "It's getting late. While this has been a blast, I should get Isabelle home and at least a little settled."

Her daughter stood and bid everyone goodbye with hugs and expressions of gratitude. "This was really fun. Thank you."

Ava smiled. "I think you're going to enjoy living on Maui, sweetheart. We're so happy you are here."

In the car, Vanessa voiced the same.

Isabelle sat in the passenger seat with her arms crossed tightly across her chest. "I don't believe you."

"Honey, why would you say that? Of course, I'm glad you're here with me."

She turned and gave her mother an angry stare. "Really? From what I hear, you never wanted me."

Vanessa's head began to pound. It was late, and she wasn't

prepared for another complicated discussion. "That's not true," she argued.

Isabelle turned and looked at her. "Yeah? Dad said you never wanted kids. That I was an oops baby late in life, and you fled and left me with him the first chance you got so you could focus on your stupid career."

Vanessa's blood boiled hearing those words out of her daughter's mouth. Clark had done a real number on both of them. Her daughter had paid the price. Still, bashing her father in return would do Isabelle no good.

She drew a long, slow breath before starting what she needed to say. "Isabelle, please listen carefully. You were a surprise, but never a mistake." She felt a lump form in her throat. "I love you. I've always loved you."

"But you loved your job more." Her daughter's voice sounded tiny.

"I'm not sure you understand the whole story. I made mistakes, but they had nothing to do with my love for you." She held her breath, knowing this was only the start of what would, no doubt, be a long journey to reclaim her daughter's trust.

She reached across the seat and took her daughter's hand. "I intend to prove that to you."

14

The door opened and Katie walked into the Pali Maui offices carrying her purse and a smile. "I'm going to the bookstore. Do either of you want to go with me?"

Ava shook her head. "I'm going to meet with Mig in a few minutes. Now that we're back to our full-time production schedule after the storm damage, he's recommending adding more employees, primarily field workers so we can run more shifts." She smiled. "But you girls go. Have a good time."

Christel shook her head. "Nope. Can't. Quarterly taxes are due next week."

Ava stood and wagged her finger. "Okay, I'm not the accountant here, but I know enough to remind you that most of what gets pulled into those tax reports is automated. Knowing you, you've checked those numbers over and again." She smiled. "Honey, you've been working far too many hours lately. Go!" she urged. "You'll be more productive in the long run if you balance your life with a little fun."

Ava turned to Katie. "I swear, between your sister and her husband's driven work schedules, I don't know when they see each other anymore." She turned and gave Christel a slight smile, an indication that she had noticed the drift. "Life is all about choices, girls."

Christel waved her hands in surrender. "Fine. I'll go." Then, under her breath, "It's not like I'll get much done around here with all the observation."

Both Ava and Katie ignored her grumblings. Instead, they both gave her a wide smile. "Good choice," her mother stated, grabbing and pushing her purse into her hands. "Have fun!"

"We will," Katie said, nearly pushing Christel out the door. "You're going to love this bookstore," she promised. "It's new."

"Yeah? Where?"

"It's in Lahaina. The name *Whale of a Read* is a bit corny, but they have a fabulous selection. I typically read e-books, but lately, I've been drawn to turning the physical pages, know what I mean?" She scowled and started the engine. "Guess you don't."

Christel fastened her seat belt. "What does that mean? I read. A lot."

"What's the last novel you picked up and read?"

Christel thought a moment. A friend had given her a copy of Fifty Shades of Grey a few years ago but she'd tucked it away, unread. Spicy books were not her thing.

"See? You can't even remember."

Katie's smug look irritated Christel to no end. It wasn't like she sat around twiddling her thumbs. She was a busy woman with loads of responsibility—obligations she'd set aside to attend this little shopping foray.

The bookstore was located a block from the coastline tucked away in a strip mall. Despite the obscure location, the shop front was adorable, if not a bit funky looking. The anterior wall was painted seafoam green. The facia was hot pink and yellow. Over the entrance was a thatched roof with artificial palm fronds and brightly-colored hibiscus blooms attached to the pillars. To the right of the door, the signage made clear that a portion of all proceeds was donated to the local library.

"Cute, huh?" Katie said, dragging her sister inside. "Are you on TikTok? They carry a lot of the books on #BookTalk."

Katie immediately ditched Christel and headed for the romance aisle, leaving Christel to wander on her own. She fingered some books on the front table display, taking in the wonderful smell of new books while opening the front covers and reading the blurbs on the back. She picked up a couple and put them back. Domestic thrillers seemed popular but who wanted to read about a psycho husband stalking and wanting to kill his wife? Books featuring billionaires were abundant. She'd pass.

Finally, she noticed a book with a mountain lodge and three women on the cover. The Sun Valley series. Hmm...she'd always wanted to visit Sun Valley, Idaho. Christel tucked the paperback under her arm and then wandered the aisles looking for her sister.

That's when she discovered a little corner in the rear of the store. The area was designated for "Little Whales" and there was a woman with gray hair and reading glasses parked on the tip of her nose reading to a small group of children who looked to be in ages ranging from four to seven, or so.

Their little faces were rapt with attention as the woman read to them in the voice of an animated tomato talking about being kind and generous and how to be a good friend.

"Those are Veggie Tales books," Katie whispered as she came up behind her. "Noelle loves them."

Christel couldn't seem to pull her eyes away from a tiny girl with her hair pulled back in a yellow bow. She sat with her dimpled hands folded in the lap of her dress, grinning from ear to ear.

"You ready?" Katie whispered.

"Huh? Oh, yeah. Sure." Christel turned but not without

looking back at the little girl. Secretly, she'd hoped her first child would be a girl.

Outside, Katie confronted her. "It'll happen you know."

"What?" Christel climbed into the passenger side of the car and closed the door. She placed the pink and white checked paper bag holding her book purchase on the floor next to her feet, along with her purse.

"I think you and Evan are trying too hard. To get pregnant, I mean." She pushed the ignition button and the engine roared to life. "You hear anecdotal stories every day of people who try and try and never conceive. Once they give up...voila!"

"Voila?"

Christel swallowed and tried not to feel angry toward her sister. She meant well, as did the many people who had mentioned something similar lately, in various ways. They all meant well.

Frankly, none of them understood what it was like to feel like a failure, to feel like you are letting your spouse down with each passing month.

"How are you and Evan?" Katie asked, eying her sideways from the driver's seat.

Christel gritted her teeth against her sister's prying questions, dodging what seemed like an invasion of her privacy. "Fine."

"Really? Because Mom and I were talking and it seems you guys are hardly ever together. I agree with what Mom said earlier. There is more to life than work. You have to nurse a relationship. Especially with your spouse."

Okay, now Katie was crossing the line.

"Who died and made you a marriage counselor?" she challenged.

"Why are you so testy about the subject?" her sister countered.

"Okay, truce. I get it. You don't want to talk about your issues with Evan."

Christel nearly snarled. "There are no issues with Evan."

Katie would not be deterred. "Look, I've been married a while. Jon and I have run into bumps many times, with many more to come, no doubt. It's important you recognize the subtle changes in your relationship early and nip the situation in the bud." She pulled into traffic and steered, heading south on Front Street. "It may be time for a little surprise."

Christel wished she could change the subject already. Knowing her sister, that would be impossible. The trick was to play along and steer the conversation into safer waters without Katie realizing what was happening. "What kind of surprise?" She dug in her purse and grabbed a pack of gum and offered it to her sister.

Katie shook her head. "No thanks." She glanced in her rearview mirror. "I think you should plan a special overnight trip. Don't tell Evan anything about your plans beforehand. Just let him come home to a packed suitcase by the door. When he asks, tell him you're not going to reveal the destination until you arrive. Make it fun. Make it spontaneous. Put some excitement back into things at home." She paused. "And pack a sexy nightgown. That's a must. That's what I do when I need to make a point with Jon."

Her sister had the nerve to wink.

If it would make her shut up already, Christel would play along. "Yeah, great idea." She reached and turned on the radio, signaling the conversation was over.

15

Christel tried not to scowl as she folded the new black satin camisole with see-through lace. Few times did she follow Katie's advice, and she would never admit to doing so now, but things had grown stale between her and Evan. Her mom and sister were right. They both worked too many hours. Add the stress of disappointment, and...well, a couple who had been married less than a year shouldn't be acting like simple roommates.

She'd booked a room at the Four Seasons Wailea, a gorgeous and very expensive resort on the island. It had seemed a silly way to spend money, but she'd reminded herself they could afford it. Besides, they were worth the cost.

Christel snapped the luggage closed, smiling to herself. Evan would have no idea that she'd packed for the both of them and taken care of every detail, including having chocolate-covered strawberries and chilled champagne waiting for them in the suite she'd reserved that overlooked a scene of water and the tops of swaying palms.

Had they more time, she would've shuttled him off to the mainland for ten days. Once, when she was going to school in

Chicago, she and some girlfriends took an extended weekend trip to Mackinac Island. The location was quaint with the car-free streets full of horse-drawn carriages, charming shop fronts with hanging pots of red and pink geraniums and blue lobelia, and the best fudge she'd ever eaten in her entire life. It was on her bucket list to take Evan there. Unfortunately, they needed to plan ahead to pull a trip of that nature off, given their work commitments.

Until then, this surprise overnighter would have to do.

As Katie recommended, Christel had kept her plans quiet, intending to surprise her husband. The minute he walked in the door, he'd spot the suitcases and the smile on her face.

Surprisingly, Christel was filled with anticipation.

The past weeks had been difficult. Both of them had quit focusing on their relationship. Instead, they'd quietly tucked away the discouragement that came with every negative test and had retreated into their work corners.

She already knew the danger in that approach. So often, she'd wished she had confronted Jay earlier in their marriage about his drinking. She supposed she'd hoped the problem would simply resolve itself, but as she'd learned...the big issues never do. Like untreated cancer, marital problems fester and can spread into all areas of your life until no remedies remain. You have no choice but to succumb to the demise of your relationship, walking away bitter and emotionally bloodied. Dead inside.

Christel wheeled the suitcase into the living room, vowing she would never allow that to happen again. This marriage would be different. This time she would nip problems in the bud before they grew.

She positioned the bag in front of the door and headed for the kitchen for some water. Before she could retrieve a glass from the cupboard, she heard Evan's engine in the driveway.

An immediate smile formed as she quickly returned to the

living room. She didn't want to miss the expression on his face when he opened the door and learned of her surprise.

"What's this?" Evan asked with raised eyebrows.

"I thought we could use a little getaway, some time together without disruption and all the outside world poking at us. We haven't done anything like this since we got married." She looked at him with expectation. "Are you surprised?"

The thought hit her that he might not appreciate an unexpected trip. He didn't know she'd called Evelyn and made sure his schedule was cleared. Besides, it was only an overnighter.

Her worries were quickly put to rest.

"I love this," he told her, drawing her into his arms. "I can't believe you did all this for us."

She brushed a kiss across her husband's cheek and whispered, "Just wait until you see the nightie tucked inside that suitcase."

Evan grinned. "Fair warning. You might not be wearing it long."

He kissed her. A real kiss, unlike the obligatory ones they'd fallen into the habit of putting up with.

Christel filled with delight. She'd have to put her pride aside and thank Katie for the idea.

The Four Seasons was everything the brochures described and more. Luxury abounded from the glossy floors in the lobby leading to an exquisitely tiled outdoor lanai with a fountain pool. Beyond that, spanning ocean views and blue sky reached as far as the eye could see.

Christel had booked dinner reservations at Spago, the famed restaurant owned by master chef Wolfgang Puck.

Evan tipped the parking attendant before weaving his fingers with her own. Together, they headed for the reservation counter, which spanned the length of the front foyer. Vases of birds of paradise were nestled at both ends of the length of shiny granite.

A perky young Asian woman greeted them with a smile. "May I help you?"

They got checked in, and the girl handed them each a room card. "I hope you enjoy your stay. Please let us know if there is anything you need."

They turned to see a familiar figure crossing the lobby heading in their direction.

Christel's breath caught.

"What is it?" Evan asked.

Under her breath, she whispered, "Mia."

Evan was well aware of the story of Mia and Christel's dad and the hurt his wife still carried. "Just be pleasant and move on," he cautioned.

Her husband was right. This was all going far too well to allow that Jezebel to ruin things. So, she lifted her chin and simply nodded as Mia neared.

"Christel? Evan?"

Drat! She would have to say something.

Thankfully, Evan intercepted. "Hello, Mia. How are you?" he said in an amiable tone.

Christel squeezed his hand in a signal not to invite further conversation.

"Are you staying with us tonight?"

"Yes," Evan confirmed. Thankfully, he didn't let on. What she and her husband chose to do was none of Mia's business.

"Do you work here now? I understood you were with one of the resorts in Kaanapali."

Christel squeezed his hand again. He could stop anytime now.

Mia nodded. "I did. When my Makuahine was diagnosed with cancer, I returned from the mainland to help take care of her. Unfortunately, there was no longer a position available. I was fortunate to land something at the Four Seasons."

"Well, congratulations," he told her.

Mia avoided Christel's gaze. "Well, please enjoy your evening. Let the front desk know if there is anything that would make your stay more comfortable."

She moved on.

Christel waited until she was out of hearing distance before she turned her full attention on Evan. "Really? We had to be that cordial?"

He laughed at her. "As opposed to being awful to her?"

She caved. He was right, of course. Still, it was never easy to encounter her former best friend, aka her father's mistress.

Their room was lovely, exceeding her expectations, with glass doors opening to a lanai overlooking the ocean in the distance and the pool area below.

"Wow," Evan said. "Look at that view."

She grabbed her husband's hand and pulled him to her. "We're not here for the scenery."

CHRISTEL LEANED against the pillows while listening to the shower run. She smiled, remembering the past hour and her time with Evan. It'd been far too long since they had gone to the place where it was all hands and moans and tongues and sweat. A slight tingle went up her spine, even thinking about how passionate they'd been.

Absolutely nothing could feel better.

She threw the covers back and climbed from the bed. With a grin, she made her way to the shower doors, opened them, and climbed inside.

"Well, well...look who came to visit," Evan said with his own wide grin splayed over that gorgeous face.

Christel ran her hand along his wet back. "Thought you could use some company."

He reached for her when his phone sounded from the bathroom counter. "Was that my phone?" he asked, shutting off the water.

"I'm not sure, but whomever it is can wait." She reached for the water handle.

He pulled a towel from the rack and stepped from the shower. Christel let her hand drop, disappointed.

Evan slid his finger across the face of his phone and pulled it to his ear. "Yeah?"

His eyebrows pulled into a frown as he listened to the voice from the other end. "Compound fracture?" He nodded and shook his head. "Crushed elbow? Sounds bad. I'm about forty-five minutes out, but have the team prepare the kid for surgery. Tell the parents not to worry."

He turned to her. "Motorcycle accident. A teenager going too fast and sideswiped a parked car after losing control. Sounds bad. I've got to go."

Christel scowled. "Can't another surgeon handle it?"

"There is no other surgeon."

"What would happen if you were on vacation and unable to drop everything and race to the hospital? What then?" she challenged.

"Don't be like that." He pulled on his pants and zipped them. "I'll try to get back."

"But what about our dinner reservations?" Christel felt unexpected anger swell. "You're just going to ditch me to eat alone?"

Evan gave her a patient look. "I'm a surgeon, Christel."

"A surgeon with crappy priorities. Yes, someone is hurt and needs medical attention. I'm not so sure it has to be you who drops everything and goes. Contrary to what you'd like everyone to believe, you are not the only physician on the island capable of running to the rescue."

He glared at her. "What's that supposed to mean?"

A silent warning went off inside her. She needed to take a

step back. Emotions were taking over; this was not where she wanted things to go. Yet, it was as if someone had lifted a gate, and weeks of buildup came flooding inside. She didn't want to let it go. She had let it go in her first marriage far too many times. She'd suffered for it.

"I don't want you to go." She swallowed and watched his face.

"You're making a crisis out of nothing here," he told her. "I'll be back when I can." He turned and toweled off his hair before reaching for the stick of deodorant on the bathroom counter.

His response, while expected, still stunned her.

For weeks, she'd been trying to hide from all the fear and the crap; the night sweats when she'd wake from a deep sleep, unable to shake the mental image of a plastic wand with no line. Her spirit was heavy with a blanket of belief that she was half a woman because she couldn't get pregnant. No amount of hiding saved her from the terror that crept into the pit of her stomach when she allowed herself to consider that she may never be a mother. Or what would happen to her marriage if she failed to give Evan a child.

Some would argue that she was putting this pressure on herself. Even so, the pressure was unbearable.

Christel wanted to find a way to express all of that to Evan and make him understand that she wasn't simply creating a crisis out of thin air. She was fighting for a lifeline.

Sometimes words fail.

"Just go then," she said, giving in.

He capped the deodorant and tossed it to the counter before turning. He planted a kiss on the top of her head. "I'll text and let you know how it's going."

16

Katie sat in the passenger side of Vanessa's car and looked up from the Maui Today article on the phone nestled in her lap. "After reading this article, I think the key to today's interview is to stay positive and take a broad approach. Don't let them box you into taking narrow positions when it's not necessary. Especially when it comes to anything relating to property taxes."

Vanessa gripped the steering wheel a little tighter and nodded. "Yeah, good advice."

Surprisingly, Vanessa felt nervous. She'd been in front of the cameras plenty of times, but always to report on someone else's story, never to advocate for herself and her electability. She had less than eight weeks to convince the residents of Maui that she could do a better job than Jim Kahale. She needed to ace this election. This interview was critical to that happening.

Katie clicked off her phone, then bent and retrieved a clipboard from the bag at her feet. "Okay, let's go over the issues again and rehearse where you stand."

Her niece had been a surprising and effective addition to the campaign team. She took her responsibilities seriously and had spent hours researching and studying what mattered to voters. Armed with Katie's input, Vanessa had been able to form the proper communication and direct a message that would hit at the core of what the constituents most cared about in this election.

"Thank you, Katie."

Her niece smiled. "For what?"

"For covering my back. You are amazing; you know that?"

Katie beamed. "Yup, I am amazing."

"No, really. Have you ever considered coming on board full-time if I'm elected? I'd make sure you were paid well."

Katie let a slow grin form. "That's so flattering, Aunt Vanessa. And tempting. It's probably no secret to those around me that I struggle to fill my days with meaning and purpose... especially when I see others who seem to be doing so much more with their time. Frankly, all that is a struggle for me. Sometimes I forget to remind myself that I do have purpose. I have a job that is far more important. Everything else must be squeezed in around that priority."

Vanessa checked her side mirror. "Why couldn't you do both?"

Katie sat up a little straighter. "This season of my life is focused on being the best mother I can be to my two girls. True, motherhood can be hard, challenging, and sometimes isolating." Her gaze drifted to her lap and the image of her girls on the screen of her phone. "But I'm the one who helps Willa and Noelle navigate life, learn skills to get along with others, and gain the support they need to be successful in life. There are tons of voices out there wanting to mold my children... messages infused with garbage and beliefs that will hurt them. My influence is essential to counter that. The time I invest in protecting and sheltering them is critical. My guidance will protect my girls and help them know how special they are. Under my direction, they will learn to make good choices. If I do my job right, Willa and Noelle will grow to be amazing and happy women."

Katie looked back at Vanessa. "While I share the parenting with Jon, being the girls' mom will always be my most important job. Sadly, it's temporary. Despite my desire, they will grow up and no longer need me. At least not like that." She laughed. "So, can I take a raincheck on that offer? Say, about a dozen years or so down the road?"

Vanessa let what her niece said sink in, absorbing the message. How could someone half her age be so wise?

Perhaps Katie didn't intend to pierce her heart, but the words stabbed at her conscience. A dull ache formed deep inside as she considered her own failures in that department.

While Isabelle's return to her life had come at an inopportune time, when she needed to focus all her time and energy on her campaign…there was no missing the fact that her daughter needed her.

Vanessa had nearly missed her chance. Now, she'd been blessed with another opportunity to connect with Isabelle.

What did that mean?

She was in the middle of a critical campaign, at a crossroads. Her professional life had been sliding, and this was her chance to change that. Winning this election could be the start of something brand new. She would be respected again. She would no longer be teetering financially.

Even more? She was good at this. In the short period she'd worked for Jim prior to everything going south, she'd discovered that ninety percent of politics was successful messaging. The key was finding out what mattered to voters and focusing on making a promise to deliver just that. Few were as skilled at ferreting out the undercurrents of what remained unsaid and using that to her advantage, especially when it came to urging donations.

She wanted to be a good mother to her daughter, and she wanted to be the next state senator from Maui.

No matter what, Vanessa knew she'd simply have to pull off the impossible and make quality time for both.

"Ms. Hart, what would you say is the most important issue facing the voters on Maui right now?"

Vanessa's gaze drifted to Katie, who stood in the shadows behind the bright lights and camera. She leaned forward and let a smile appear. "Frank, I don't need to tell your viewers how rising gas and grocery prices, increased property taxes and managing our tourism industry remain at the forefront of voters' minds, and my own. What I think no one else in this race is saying is that there are solutions to these problems. Sadly, my opponent is not embracing any of these solutions."

"And you are."

She nodded confidently. "Yes. For example, I've teamed up with a biodiesel company known for championing climate sustainability and economic diversification. In our meetings, they've voiced many viable alternatives for approaching these issues. You see, Frank, I listen carefully to those who have ideas, the kinds of people who aren't afraid to think out of the box. New times, new issues...well, they demand new approaches and ideas."

Vanessa smiled to herself. She could almost see the people on the other side of that camera nodding. She could kiss Katie for finding that information and following up, adding the arrow to her quiver of ways to target voters and land this election squarely in her lap.

"So, would you consider yourself a conservative or a progressive?"

Vanessa drew a deep breath, and let her expression turn

serious. "I believe those labels are damaging and erect walls that divide. I am a resident of Maui, and a fellow dweller on this beautiful island. I'm blessed to serve my friends and neighbors, if they will put me in a position to do so."

The interviewer flipped a page fastened to his clipboard. "One last question."

She nodded. Bring it; she thought, knowing she was acing this broadcast.

"It was brought to our attention recently that your daughter had a little..." He paused and coughed into his fist. "Well, a little run-in with the law."

Vanessa tensed. Her mind raced. She'd spent hours with Frank leading up to this live interview. She thought she'd properly molded him into fully supporting her. She was wrong.

As a practiced news anchor, she knew how these things went. She wasn't entirely surprised.

"Frank, it may surprise you to discover I'm glad you brought that up."

His eyebrows lifted.

"You see, the most important job any woman can have is being a mother. True, motherhood can be hard, challenging, and sometimes isolating." Her gaze drifted to her interviewer, and she locked eyes with him. "Fathers play an important role, but as Isabelle's mother, I am the one who helps her navigate life, learn skills to get along with others, and gain the support she needs to be successful in life. That is critically so when a child makes a bad choice. I'm the one who has to steer her back on course."

Vanessa lifted her chin and crossed her wrists in her lap. "There are tons of voices out there wanting to mold our children...messages infused with garbage and beliefs that will hurt them. Many of my voters are mothers just like me. We know that our influence is essential to counter that. The time we invest in protecting and sheltering our youth is critical. Our guidance will protect Maui's children and help them know how special they are. Under our direction, they will learn to make good choices."

Now she looked directly into the camera. "While I sincerely hope to be the next state senator from Maui, my daughter will always be my top priority. If I do my job right and steer Isabelle's future, she will not let this one mistake take her under."

Vanessa let her face break into a wide smile. "Instead, she'll grow up to be an amazing and happy woman, a proud and contributing citizen here on Maui. Perhaps someday, even a candidate for an elected office."

She let out the breath she'd been holding and directed her focus behind the camera.

Katie frowned and locked eyes with Vanessa, who quickly looked away. Okay, yes...she'd taken Katie's message and made it her own. By doing so, she'd also just connected with half the voters on Maui in a way Jim Kahele never could.

17

Christel leaned into the hotel bathroom mirror and applied lipstick, a pretty shade of coral that perfectly matched the flowers on the beach dress she'd splurged on when she'd decided to surprise Evan with this overnight trip—a surprise ruined by his quick exit.

She sighed, put the cap on the lipstick, and then took a step back. She looked really good. Not that it mattered much now.

When Evan decided to return to the hospital, she had two choices. She could bag the stay, pack, and go home. Or, she could stay and use her dinner reservation even if she had to dine alone. She could always download a good book and spend time reading while enjoying Wolfgang Puck's world-class recipes.

The Four Seasons hotel was billed as a luxury hotel for good reason. The décor was a feast for the eyes, the attention of the hotel staff unsurpassed, and the dining indescribable. Tourists made reservations for Spago months in advance just so they could sample the first-class selections.

Christel was seated at a linen-draped table near the open-air lanai overlooking the ocean. The flames from the tiki torches illuminated tall palms swaying in the gentle evening breeze. Pots filled with rare tropical blooms fragranced the sweet air and mixed with the aroma of the salty ocean.

The entire experience was heady and romantic.

Christel ignored the sympathetic look from the suited maître d as he handed a single menu across the table. She thanked him and scanned the selections, finally deciding on roasted Hapu'upu'u—snow crab crust with horseradish potato puree and lemon-caper meuniere. She also ordered a side of Molokai sweet yam with coconut sauce.

"And to drink, ma'am?"

"Champagne, please."

The waiter nodded. "Glass?"

"Bottle. The most expensive you have." Christel knew she was being indulgent. She didn't care. It was a small price for Evan to pay for ruining her romantic evening.

When served, the food was everything it was said to be. She enjoyed every morsel and felt a little tipsy from the bubbly champagne. Thank goodness she only had to head up to her room when the meal was over.

"Christel?"

She looked up, and immediately a scowl formed. "Mia." Her response was short and terse, definitely not an invitation for further discourse.

Mia glanced at the empty chair on the other side of the table.

"Evan was called to the hospital. An emergency," Christel explained, immediately chastising herself for feeling the need to supply unwarranted information. The champagne was going to her head.

"I'm sorry," Mia said.

Christel hated admitting it, but her former best friend looked stunning. Her simple white one-shoulder dress hung casually at her ankles, adorned with sandals with simple gold straps. Small gold palm leaves hung from her ears which matched stacks of gold bangles on her wrist. The look was amazing and offset her straight, long jet-black hair.

It was easy to see how any man would be pulled in—even her father.

The notion immediately made Christel feel cross.

"If you don't mind, I'm…" She motioned to her now-empty plate, aware of how snotty her voice sounded.

Tears sprouted in Mia's eyes.

Tears!

Christel didn't bother to hide a heavy sigh. "Really?" she challenged.

She slapped her linen napkin onto the table. "What do you expect, Mia? You are oh-so-sorry, and now you deserve all your relationships with our family to be restored?"

Mia dabbed her middle fingertip at the corners of her eyes. "No. I—"

"Save it," Christel hissed. "I don't care that my mother is showing you forgiveness. To me, you are persona non gratis. You mean nothing to me anymore."

The maître d scurried over. "Do we have a problem?"

Mia laid her elegant hand on his forearm. "No, Enrique. All is well."

She raised her chin. "Christel, there is no further way I can express my sorrow over my past choices and what they did to you and your family. Nothing is more gut-wrenching than knowing this kind of shame. Knowing you've lost something precious at your own hand and that no matter what you do, restoration will never come." Her eyes turned soft. "I only hope you never find yourself facing the same."

18

"Mom! How could you?"

"Baby, listen." Vanessa reached for her daughter's hand. "Let me explain."

"Let you explain? Are you kidding?" Isabelle huffed and pulled away. "I am not fodder for your campaign. Don't you dare make yourself out to be Mother of the Year and discuss anything about me—not in public, or anywhere else for that matter!"

Vanessa groaned inside. Somehow, she'd done it again. She'd pushed her daughter away.

"Baby, I'm sorry. I won't," she promised, already wondering how she would keep that commitment when she knew the incident with Isabelle's indiscretion in Seattle would likely be brought up again. She'd simply have to brainstorm with Katie and come up with a better response, one that did not cause Isabelle further disdain for her mothering skills.

Unfortunately, her daughter's contempt was shared by her father.

"What were you thinking?" Clark barked over the phone when he called later that night.

"Excuse me; I believe you forfeited the right to critique my life when you signed the divorce papers." Her ex-husband had some nerve butting in and voicing his opinion without any invitation to do so.

"I did not forfeit my right to weigh in on anything that affects our daughter."

"Oh, that's classic. Especially when you didn't have time for her *and* your new trophy wife. Besides, you have real nerve criticizing me when it was on your watch that she got in trouble."

She could nearly hear him growl across the phone. "Look, keep her out of the public light. I mean it. Just because you choose to climb on stage and say 'Look at me' doesn't mean our daughter needs to be dragged up there with you."

"Look at me? Why you pompous—"

"I mean it, Vanessa. If forced, I will change my mind about her staying with you." He paused, but only to gain steam. "I will fly over there and get her if I need to."

"Are you threatening me?"

"Yes."

"Bite me!" she screamed before sliding her finger across the button to end the call.

She was shaking with anger as she tossed the phone to the kitchen counter. Thank goodness Isabelle was over at Ava's and did not hear that exchange. Given her earlier stance, she would no doubt take her dad's side in this. All she needed was for the two of them to team up and fight her.

Vanessa kicked off her heels and grabbed a bottle of water from the refrigerator. She unscrewed the cap and took a long drink.

Okay, yes. She hadn't really thought through what she'd said on camera. She didn't need Clark's disapproval to tell her what Isabelle had already revealed.

Vanessa leaned against the counter and pondered her next move. Suddenly, an idea formed.

She downed the water, then tossed the empty bottle into the trash receptacle before heading for her scattered shoes. After wedging her feet into the pumps, she grabbed her purse from the counter and headed for the door...smiling.

AIDEN HUNG up his uniform jacket before clocking out. He was on the way out to the parking lot when his phone rang.

"Hey, Christel. What's up?"

"I just ran into Mia," she reported. "She had the nerve to stop by my table at Spago just to...I don't know...say hi."

Aiden scowled. "Christel, have you been drinking?"

"Maybe a little," she admitted.

Concern welled. "Don't drive. I'll come get you."

"I don't need rescued, baby brother. I'm at the Four Seasons in Wailea."

"The Four Seasons? Alone?"

Christel recounted the entire story to him, bemoaning the fact that her husband left her for a medical emergency. He knew it would be dangerous to voice that he took his brother-in-law's side in this. He understood how emergencies tended to pop up at inopportune times.

As if realizing the same thing, Christel hiccupped and said, "Like I'm going to convince you how rude that is. I mean, I have this great room, and I'm sitting here all by myself."

"I'm sorry, Christel. Sounds rough." He wasn't sure his sister would catch the sarcasm in his voice.

"Hey! I know. Why don't you come over here? It's still early. I'll have room service deliver another bottle of champagne to the room. And food, if you're hungry."

"Sounds like you might need to have some coffee delivered instead."

"Oh, don't be a party poop. I already have one of those in

my life. Just get over here." She cited the room number, and the phone clicked off, not giving him a chance to decline.

Forty minutes later, he stood in front of his sister's hotel room. He knocked, hoping the champagne she'd drank earlier hadn't knocked her out. If she failed to answer, he supposed he could always wander down to the bar and grab a bite before heading home.

The door swung open. "There you are. Took you long enough." She waved him inside. A silver bucket with a dark green bottle perched inside was on the table. Two flutes were beside the bucket.

He leaned and inspected the scene.

"Those are frozen grapes inside the flutes," she reported. "Further chills the champagne without adding ice."

Aiden nodded. "Well, learn something every day."

His sister expertly popped the cork on the bottle and filled the glasses, handing one off to him. "C'mon," she said, motioning for the bed.

Christel stacked the pillows against the headboard, sat, and patted the place beside her. She grabbed the remote. "Want to watch a movie?"

He sat on the edge of the bed beside her.

She took a sip of her champagne. "I have dinner coming. It should be here..." She glanced at her watch. "In fifteen."

He grinned and maneuvered himself in place on top of the ice-blue coverlet. "What am I having?"

"Japanese Waygu steak. With tempura asparagus. Oh, and I ordered us both Kula strawberry cream puffs. Made with real whipped cream."

"I thought you ate already," he teased.

His sister grinned back at him. "There's always room for real whipped cream."

She clicked on the television and scrolled to the movie options. "What are you in the mood for?"

They settled on Crazy Asian Love, a romantic comedy she claimed she'd already seen but loved enough to watch again. They were barely five minutes into the film when she turned to him. "So, Shane says you went out on a date recently?"

Aiden groaned. "Yeah, it didn't go so well."

He told her about the fiasco and the girl who left the contents of her stomach at his feet. "Pretty sad when you have to pack a bottle of Pepto Bismol when you go out."

Christel laughed so hard that she nearly choked. "Stop. You're killing me." She paused the movie.

"You think it's funny? I had sliders on."

Christel doubled over with laughter. "Stop. I'm going to wet the bed."

Aiden and Christel talked and laughed. It had been a long time since the two of them had shared time together. Aiden missed that. He told her so. "We have to do this more often, sis."

A sound at the door interrupted his plan to tell her how much she meant to him.

Christel popped up off the bed and went for the door. She pulled it open, and there stood Evan with a key fob in his hand.

"Sorry, couldn't get this blasted thing to work." He surveyed the room and greeted his brother-in-law with a nod. "Uh...am I interrupting?"

Christel flung her arms around her husband's neck and hiccupped. "Absolutely not, my love. The more men in my bed, the merrier!"

19

Vanessa rapped lightly on her daughter's bedroom door. When there was no answer, she pushed the door open and peered inside. Isabelle was on the bed with her attention buried in her iPad.

"Honey?" Vanessa stepped further inside. "Isabelle?"

Her daughter glanced up and ignored her.

Vanessa motioned for her to remove her earbuds.

Isabelle didn't move.

Frustrated yet holding back her irritation, Vanessa moved to the side of the bed and gently lifted the iPad from her daughter's hands. She motioned for the earbud removal again.

This time her daughter complied.

"I have a surprise for you," Vanessa announced. "Get dressed and meet me out at the car." She ventured a look that clearly expressed a warning not to mess with her and ignore the directive.

Vanessa returned to the living room, where she hesitated by the door. She waited.

Finally, Isabelle appeared. She was dressed in loose-fitting cropped jeans, a tank top, and flip-flops.

Vanessa tossed a bag into her arms. "You may want to put this on."

Her daughter's eyes lifted. "What is it?"

"New swimming shorts and a coordinating long-sleeve rash guard top." Before her daughter could respond, she pushed a bottle of sunscreen into her hands.

"I have my own sunscreen."

"This brand is reef safe and doesn't contain harmful ingredients to corals, fish, and marine wildlife." Vanessa turned for the door. "I'll be in the car. Hurry, I have an important dinner tonight, so we don't have time to dilly-dally."

A few minutes later, Isabelle wandered out the front door.

"Don't forget to lock it," her mother called out from the car.

Isabelle approached and opened the passenger side door. She was ready to slip inside when she stopped. "I thought you were alone."

"Hey, Isabelle," Willa said from the back seat. "This is Kina Aka, my good friend. Your mom came and picked us up. She's going to take us snorkeling."

A tiny smile formed on her daughter's face. "Oh, cool." She climbed inside and snapped her seat belt.

"Kina is the girl I told you about at Nana's the other night."

Kina nodded. "Yeah, we do stuff together all the time. I was excited when Willa told me her cousin had moved to the island. We'll have to hang out."

That seemed to be all it took. The girls spent the entire drive to Lahaina chattering about school, their friends, and teachers. "So, you start on Monday?" Kina asked. "Even though you're a junior, we can still meet up in the lunchroom and after class."

Vanessa smiled. Her big plan was to connect Isabelle with some girls her age, and it appeared to be working. If her daughter put down some social roots, she wouldn't be as vulnerable to leaving for Seattle and returning to her dad.

Vanessa would have a bit more leeway when traversing the bridge from evil mother to friend and confidante.

Vanessa pulled into a parking spot on Canal Street by Banyan Court. "Okay, we're here."

Isabelle climbed out of the car and looked around. "Wow, look at that tree."

"That's the Banyan," Kina told her. "It's pretty famous."

"Yeah," Willa added. "It's the largest banyan tree in the country. This one is over sixty feet high."

A rooster darted across their path.

Isabelle's eyes widened. "Wow. I'm not in Seattle anymore."

"Tell us about Seattle," Willa urged as the girls followed Vanessa to the boat dock.

"Well, we have Pike Place Market. Lots of fun vendors set up shop, and there's an open-air fish stand where men are known to fling large salmon or tuna in the air."

"Really? That's *so* judge." Kina swung her bag at her side while walking. "Have you ever gone up in the Space Needle?"

Isabelle nodded. "Lots of times. It's a bit overrated, but the observation deck is pretty great. On a clear day, you can see Mount Rainier."

Kina sighed. "I've seen pictures on the internet."

"Okay, we're here," Vanessa announced. As they neared her brother's boat, he waved.

Responding to Isabelle's confused look, Vanessa explained that her brother owned several large excursion rafts. "He takes tourists out on whale-watching and snorkeling trips," she explained. "My nephew, Shane, works for him. They are going to take us out for the day."

"Welcome aboard the Canefire," Jack greeted. He wore an open shirt that allowed his belly to protrude beyond the fabric. An unlit cigar teetered between his lips as he talked.

Vanessa quickly made introductions before motioning for

her daughter and the other two girls to board. "Are we alone?" she asked, seeing no tourists.

Her brother nodded. "Aye, aye. Captain Jack and his first mate, Shane, have planned something extraordinary for our special guests." He winked. "An exclusive excursion."

Shane helped them step onto the sizeable hard-bottom raft. He passed out snorkeling gear and helped the girls slip into their fins and goggles. For Isabelle's benefit, he gave brief instructions on how to clear the air tube.

Isabelle's face was a mixture of excitement and trepidation. She peered over the edge of the giant raft into the water. "Oh, my goodness! What is that? Is that a shark?" She stood and moved away from the edge.

Captain Jack let out a hearty laugh. "Oh, that's just a little leopard shark that hangs around. We call him Spotty. He's not dangerous." Captain Jack grinned, showing off a gold tooth. "Not unless you try to arm wrestle with him."

Isabelle took in the information but seemed to remain shaken.

Willa leaned over. "Don't worry about sharks. There aren't any in the areas where we snorkel."

This seemed to reassure Isabelle. Still, she glanced over her shoulder toward the water as she eased herself down on a bench next to Kina.

Shane pulled the line in, and Jack started up the engine. It chugged, coughed, emitted a plume of blue smoke, then roared to life. "Hang on," Jack called out over the engine's sound.

The vessel started moving and slowly glided away from the dock. Overhead, the sky was bright blue. A cool breeze blew against their faces as they crossed the water.

As soon as they passed the no wake boundary, Captain Jack gunned the motor, and the raft planed onto the water's surface. The wind blew through their hair as they picked up speed.

Captain Jack rubbed at his white beard and started his

typical spiel as they passed a double-decked boat filled with tourists. "The Canefire is the safest craft on the water. We've even rescued Coast Guard boats when they get in trouble." He patted the inflated side. "Yup, Old Grandma has to save the grandchildren once in a while."

The surf breaking against the racing vessel sounded like low thunder. As they picked up the pace, loud gusts of wind caught their hair.

Captain Jack yelled, his voice booming over top of the wind. "Keep your eyes peeled. We're heading into whale season. It's often claimed that the Pacific Ocean is the whales' living room; the waters surrounding the Hawaiian Islands the bedroom, where these magnificent creatures come to birth, raise their young, and then kick them out." He laughed and turned his cap around. His hand went to the accelerator, and he pushed the engine into a faster gear and laughed again as he clamped his teeth on the unlit cigar to keep from losing it in the wind.

It took just under an hour to reach Makena Landing. As the engine slowed, Shane downed the last of his bottled water and put the empty in the storage bin. "This is one of the best snorkeling reefs on the island." He pointed. "Just offshore of that rocky stretch of coastline that forms Nahuna Point is a dive spot known as Turtle Arches. We're definitely going to hang with a few Hono today."

He seemed as excited as the girls as he checked the straps on their life vests and helped ease them into the water. He jumped in after them and motioned for them to follow.

Vanessa turned to her brother and kissed his pock-marked tan face. "Thanks for doing this, Jack."

He let his head fall back as he let out a laugh. "No worries, girly. I live for this stuff."

Vanessa smiled at him before getting in the water. She glided through the surface toward the girls catching up with them with little effort, just in time to hear Willa instruct

Isabelle on how to simply place her face in the water and blow the air tube to clear the water if necessary. "It's easy," she promised.

Seconds later, Vanessa heard squeals. Isabelle's head popped up out of the water. She tore the mouthpiece away. "Mom! It's incredible!" She shook her head. "There are so many fish. Yellow ones. Blue and orange ones. Bunches and bunches." Clearly, her daughter was delighted. That delighted Vanessa.

She couldn't help herself. She made the couple of strokes it took to meet with Isabelle and pulled her into a wet embrace. Isabelle let her, and that made the entire day away from the campaign worth it.

"Come on," Vanessa said, motioning. "Let's see if we can find one of those turtles. I know just the place."

She led her daughter to an underground lava arch, a place her father used to take Ava and her when they were girls.

Along the way, she pointed out vibrant butterfly fish, eels, and even an elusive frog fish. As they neared the arch, they spotted their first Honu gliding along a rim of white coral. As many times as Vanessa had seen sea turtles, she remained amazed at their size. Many were as big as a small sofa table. Their hard shells were shades of green and teal. Their underbelly was more green and yellow.

Thought to live between sixty and eighty years, the Honu turtles symbolized longevity. In Hawaiian culture, their presence was considered a form of 'aumakua or ancestral spirit offering lifelong protection, wisdom, and guidance, and was said to bring good luck and peace. Since being listed as a "threatened" species in 1978, the Green Sea Turtle population had made a comeback. Even so, much care was extended to these beautiful sea creatures to preserve their presence on the islands.

Isabelle grabbed Vanessa's hand and squeezed. She reached

her other hand in front of her body toward the turtle. Snorkelers are warned never to touch, or bother, these creatures. Even so, the large Honu flapped its front flippers and glided in their direction. Feet away, the turtle stopped so close that Vanessa and Isabelle could peer into its big black eyes.

Minutes later, when they surfaced, her daughter was crying.

"I had no idea," she said, wiping her face. "Such beauty. You can see pictures, but mere images can't possibly compare to this." She turned to Vanessa. "Thanks, Mom."

"Ha, we knew you'd like it," Willa said as she approached. Kina was close behind.

Back in the boat, Isabelle couldn't quit talking about the experience. "So, you guys get to do this all the time?"

Both Willa and Kina nodded. "Yup. That's not even half the fun of living on island, Willa told her.

Kina agreed. "Wait until you swim in the water pool under Waikamoi Falls. Way boujie."

Vanessa looked over at her brother, who had moved into the helm, ready to start the engine. He winked back at her.

If there was anything Vanessa was good at, it was making a plan and devising methods to accomplish her goals. If you wanted something, you had to go after it.

She wanted her daughter back.

Today was a great first start to achieving just that.

20

Aiden pulled the Maui Emergency Services truck into the yard at the station and cut the engine. "When are novice hikers going to learn to stay on the designated paths?" he asked, shaking his head.

Meghan slipped her helmet off and let it drop into her lap. "If people started following safety rules, we'd soon be out of business." She shook her long dark hair out and pushed her aviators up on her head. "Don't know about you, but I need this job." She gave him a wink.

Inside, they were greeted by Jeremy Hogan, a coworker who happened to be one of the fastest swimmers on the rescue team. He was a former Olympic hopeful but was bumped from competition when he was in a car accident and broke his clavicle.

Some would be bitter when facing such an unfortunate situation. Jeremy simply moved on and counted it as bad luck. They were lucky to have him here at Maui Emergency Services. As captain, Aiden made sure he knew how important he was to the team.

"Hey, Captain. You have a visitor." Jeremy pointed up the

metal stairs. "She's waiting in your office."

"She?" Aiden hung up his gear on his designated hook.

"Yeah, some chick with blonde hair. I don't normally send people up to your office without you being there, but she claimed she was a good friend."

Aiden frowned. He couldn't imagine who Jeremy could be talking about. "Thanks, man," he told his teammate before bounding up the stairs, taking two at a time.

Inside his office sat a girl, her back to the door. Aiden frowned, unable to place the woman. "Hello? May I help you?"

She turned, her face instantly brightening.

Aiden nearly choked. It was that girl from the bar. The one who drank too much and got sick.

He struggled to maintain his composure, mentally telling himself he was making a new station rule: No one would be allowed upstairs unescorted...ever.

"Hey," he finally said.

She stood and turned. "Aiden." She smiled and pulled him into an embrace.

His arms remained at his side. "Uh, hey. This is a surprise."

"I had such a good time the other night. It's not often I connect with someone at that level. I wanted to stop by and see you again. Are you free tonight?" she asked, hopefully.

"No," he said quickly. "I promised my mother I would have dinner with her tonight."

"I would love to meet your mother," she offered.

Sydney Alexander looked so normal, pretty even. She wore a sundress in his favorite blue color. The tone matched her eyes. Her hair draped loosely around her shoulders, shiny, soft-looking, and the color of coffee after pouring too much cream. Upon a second look, the tone was more of a muted blonde.

Sydney batted thick lashes. "What do you say? Want to bring me along?"

Who was this chick? She had no social graces. And Aiden

had no intention of seeing her again, no matter how attractive or intellectually stimulating he'd initially found her to be. He doubted they would be discussing photography angles and the fantastic trips she'd taken to capture the perfect shot at sunset. Instead, she'd be downing alcohol until she couldn't even remember she'd lost the contents of her stomach on his shoes.

"What time?" she pushed, seeming not the least bit embarrassed by her earlier behavior.

Did she even remember?

He rubbed at the back of his neck. "Uh, as nice as that offer sounds, Sydney, I'll have to pass."

"Oh? Why?"

Her question took him back. He'd never encountered someone who continued to push when he politely declined a proposed date. He needed to find a way to shake this girl. "My mom looks forward to our evenings. We tend to keep the time saved for us to connect." He looked at her. "Sorry."

"What about after?" She grabbed her purse and slipped the strap on her shoulder. "I can meet you at your house?"

"Again, I'm sorry. I have an early morning. There's no way I can be out late."

A look of disappointment crossed her face. "What about tomorrow night?"

His mind raced to find another excuse. He didn't want to lie. He didn't want to put gasoline on this fire and watch it flame up...possibly out of control. "I'll call you," he offered, edging her to the door.

She stopped and pulled her phone from her bag. "Give me your number. I'll watch for your call."

Aiden groaned inside. Now what? No way was he going to give her his phone number. Not when every indication told him she'd use it...and often.

Her thumb scrolled. "Oh, never mind. I have it."

He scowled. "You have it? How?"

"Your brother gave it to me." She flipped around and wiggled her fingers at him. "Well, enjoy your dinner with your mom. I'll be in touch."

She started to leave, then suddenly stopped. She turned, grabbed his cheeks in her hand, and pulled his face to hers, planting an unexpected kiss...one she didn't pull back from.

Aiden nearly coughed with the surprise move, especially when whistles from below made their way through his open door.

He'd had enough. He grabbed Sydney's shoulders and moved her back. "Uh, that's not something I do here."

She had the nerve to laugh. She lightly slapped his chest. "That's what they all say."

With that, she made her way out the door and headed for the stairs, still waving over her shoulder.

21

"So, how do I look?" Vanessa twirled in front of Katie as they walked to the waiting town car at the Daniel K. Inouye International Airport in Honolulu.

Katie barely pulled her attention from the amenities as she slipped into the back seat of the town car. Plush seats. Stocked bar. Piped in music that rivaled any upscale jazz bar. "What? Uh, you look fine."

Vanessa slid in beside Katie and opened her compact to inspect her lipstick. "Well, that was astounding affirmation."

"Sorry, I—"

"Yes, because what you should have said is, 'Aunt Vanessa, you look amazing. That little black sequined number, those four-inch stilettos, the crystal chandeliers dangling from your ears—you're definitely going to own the room.'" She gave her niece a coy smile and patted her leg. "What's the matter, Katie? You've been distracted ever since we boarded the plane."

"No, it's nothing like that. It's just that I'm wondering how it will look to the voters when they learn that you are courting donors outside Maui."

Vanessa quickly waved off Katie's concern. "This is how

politics are done. Everyone knows the big money comes from off-island corporations who hold interests in Maui. I am perfectly fine accepting donations, so long as those interests do not conflict with my constituents." She gave Katie a reassuring smile. "If we work this event right, we might find our campaign coffers filling up." Her deep brown eyes twinkled. "Some very deep pockets will be attending tonight."

By deep pockets, she meant the kind of people who had the money to shore up considerable influence—especially when it came to regulatory matters that could affect their bottom lines and their shareholders.

When they arrived, their driver opened the car door, and Vanessa slid out. She waited for Katie to do the same. Together, they made their way through the massive entry and into the Grand Hall of the historic 'Iolani Palace, with its magnificent columned lobby, marble floors, and large staircase made of Hawaiian koa wood.

"Good evening, Ms. Hart. Ms. Ackerman."

Vanessa nodded at the concierge, who had done his homework and no doubt memorized the guest list. "Good evening."

The man, with his precise haircut and impeccable suit, stepped forward and directed them to the State Dining Room. "I hope your evening at the 'Iolani Palace is an enjoyable one."

"Thank you." Vanessa linked arms with Katie, and together they moved for the grand staircase.

She leaned over and whispered, "After learning this would be tonight's venue, I looked this place up on the internet. The history is impressive. The 'Iolani Palace was the only royal palace on U.S. soil and had been the residence of the rulers of the Kingdom of Hawai'i, beginning with Kamehameha III. The palace was now located in the capitol district of downtown

Honolulu and was listed on the National Register of Historic Places.

"Is that so?" Katie studied the surroundings, clearly impressed as they entered the crowded room.

Vanessa almost smiled as she waved across the room at one of her donors, a guy who owned a private jet company with its own hangar at Kahalui Airport on Maui.

This fundraiser was undoubtedly going to be a dreary repeat of dozens she'd attended before, where power mongers from throughout Hawaii brought their agendas disguised as urgent needs essential to society.

She didn't mean to sound cynical. When elected, it would be an honor to serve in the state senate, to represent constituents relying on her to make a difference. With that role came a level of influence and prestige many would consider a golden coin. But that shiny penny sometimes had a tarnished underside.

She'd covered enough news stories in politics to understand there were people who used the system for personal gain. Events like these seemed to pull them out of the woodwork, the ones who worked the angles, pressed their agendas—individuals who stopped at nothing to attain their goals, even if they had to convince themselves the ends justified the means.

Admittedly, these were her kind of people. She understood them.

She placed her hand on Katie's back and guided her through the crowded room toward a lobbyist group she'd had lunch with earlier in the week—three individuals who worked for an independent hospitality association and wanted her to vote against any upcoming bill that would impose additional regulations on beach access in sensitive marine areas.

"Ms. Hart," one of them said, extending his hand. "So glad to see you again. Have you given any thought to what we discussed earlier?"

The sole woman of the group wedged herself into the conversation. "Bill, Bill—let the poor woman and her associate get a drink first." She flashed a brilliant smile at Vanessa and Katie. "And you are?"

Her niece stepped forward. "Hello. I'm Katie Ackerman. I'm with the campaign."

Vanessa mentally smiled. Good girl. No need to diminish her role by explaining that she was family.

"So nice to meet you. I'm Barbara Zehner." The woman waved over a tuxedoed server and slid two glasses of champagne from the tray he carried and into the hands of Vanessa and Katie.

Bill, looking impatient, took a glass from the tray as well. "So, tell me, Vanessa. I'm not one to dog-whistle my politics. The figures we supplied clearly show how small hotels across the islands would have to close rather than face the liability of missing the compliance date. Do you think you could swing your support our way?"

Vanessa patted him on the shoulder. "Well, we both know that I face a fight ahead. In order to secure this election against Jim Kahale, I'm going to need financial resources." She let the statement hang in the air a few seconds before continuing. "Of course, if elected, then yes...my door would always remain open to finding solutions to the concerns you share."

Satisfaction bloomed across Bill's face. "Well, that's good news."

Katie stepped forward. "We can expect your financial help, then?"

Bill nodded enthusiastically. "Yes, of course," he said. "Just tell me where to mail the check. We need to stop this attack on small businesses."

Barbara lifted her hand and waved at someone she couldn't quite see in her line of vision.

"Well, look who's here!" The booming voice belonged to

Jim Kahale. He sidled up, drink in hand, with that new bimbo close behind. Tracy Mussman, as Katie had once pointed out, entered every situation smiling and camera ready.

With a broad smile pasted on her face, Vanessa took the power position and was first to extend her hand. "Good evening, Jim." She nodded at his new campaign manager. "Miss Mussman."

"Well, hello, Vanessa." Jim brushed her cheek with a kiss. "So good to see you this evening."

Out of the corner of her eye, she saw a camera crew break through the crowd, the glaring bright lights from the camera nearly blinding her.

"Excuse me, Mr. Kahale, Ms. Hart. Could we get a few minutes?" Without waiting for a response, a man Vanessa recognized from a local television station pointed a microphone their way. "Political pundits everywhere project that while several candidates are jumping in the race to seat Maui's next state senator, they assert that in the end, it will be the two of you in the final runoff."

While no question had yet been posed, Vanessa knew what was coming.

"Either of you care to comment?"

Jim smiled into the camera. "Well, let me just go on record right now and tell your viewers that I would be delighted to face off with this admirable opponent in the upcoming election. While our positions rarely match on many of the issues voters care so much about, Vanessa Hart is a fine young woman." A slight grin played across his face. "Unfortunately, it takes time to gain experience. Ms. Hart believes a career in news media, a job she was forcibly exited from, prepares her for a job of this magnitude and import. I simply disagree, and so will the voters on election night."

All eyes turned to Vanessa as the camera pivoted in her

direction. The sound level in the room lowered considerably as they waited for her response.

"Thank you, Jim. It's true. I believe the polls reveal Maui voters appreciate a *fresh* approach to the issues they care about. Voters appreciate a chance to turn from the tired old approaches to embrace someone who will bring new ideas to the table. That's why I left your campaign and decided to run for office myself."

Out of the corner of her eye, she saw Katie lift her chin and smile.

"As I stated, polls show my efforts are clearly hitting the mark with voters, and I can promise this." She paused for effect. "I am committed to serving the needs of the people of Maui and the State of Hawaii. I plan to win."

"Thank you, Ms. Hart." The camera pulled back.

Jim Kahale stepped forward. "Uh, just one question, if I might."

The cameraman redirected his shot.

"You have something you want to add, Mr. Kahale?" the reporter asked.

The skin around her opponent's eyes tightened. "Where do our treasured Honu turtles fit into your grand campaign plan?"

Vanessa scowled. "Excuse me?"

"Word has it you are coaxing a large donation from an organization working to block important legislation to protect our turtles." Her opponent tossed the accusation into the conversation, likely hoping to blow up Vanessa's credibility and create collateral damage.

That was what she both hated, and loved, about politics. It was a game.

May the best one win.

She cleared her throat. "If you are referring to the legislation meant to promote better access to the remote beaches, then you would be accurate." She scanned the crowd for Bill, and gave him a nod. "I will carefully weigh the concerns of everyone, create some middle ground, and form a comprehensive plan that will not implode our tourism economy while ensuring complete access to all necessary public areas for our treasured physically disabled citizens and tourists and that will protect our treasured sea life. If elected, I will form a special committee to ensure one set of interests never shoves out another."

Satisfied she'd staved off Jim's guerilla potshots, she smiled and added, "Now, you'll have to excuse us."

The following morning, media across the state ran headlines quoting what she'd said. Op-eds accused Jim Kahale of being out of touch. One popular online blog included a cartoon drawing of a beach lined by wheelchairs and turtles with this quote underneath: "I'm feeling like a swim today. How about you, Joe?"

Calls came pouring into her campaign office with statements of support. According to Katie, donations skyrocketed in the aftermath.

It seemed everyone supported her run.

All but one.

She doubted Jim Kahale was happy with any of this.

22

Christel laced up her running shoes, grabbed her water bottle, and climbed from her car. She made her way across the dirt parking area to the head of the Kahakapao Loop Trail, an upcountry pathway winding through the Makawao Forest Reserve.

Only one other car was in the parking area, a rental car. She could almost hear Evan's voice warning her about personal safety when running alone. Not to worry, she had her pepper spray tucked inside her jogging shorts and had placed an Apple air tag inside her jog bra to ensure she could be tracked in case of emergencies. Maui was known to be a low-crime area, but she didn't want to take safety for granted.

Overhead, a canopy of quiet forest and draping hinahina, a silvery-gray moss hanging from the tree limbs, provided shade and a sanctuary for birds to cheer her on as she made her way toward the summit. She loved the solitude as her shoes padded against the packed dirt. Here, she could think...refocus.

Lately, she and Evan had begun to argue.

She hated conflict. She hated the building rift in their relationship even more.

Worse, she knew much of the angst was caused by her irritation.

Evan was gone...a lot. She tired of eating dinner alone, waking up to him rushing out the door before the break of dawn for an early morning surgery, or trying to delve into a deep and meaningful conversation while he had his head buried in some online article on the most recent developments in stainless steel intramedullary rods used in spinal fixation.

Flexibility was her superpower. Long ago, she learned to juggle the demands of school, work, family...and personal stress. But enough was enough.

"Evan," she'd told him while lying in bed in the dark. "I'm lonely. Marrying you was supposed to change all that."

He immediately reached for her. "Oh, babe. I don't know what to say. I love you. You know that."

She swallowed her tears. She did know that. She also knew the toll that difficult things could have on a marriage.

Lately, there were times when they needed to talk, yet the words would never come. There were times when they needed to understand, yet they didn't always know how. With the growing disappointment over the negative pregnancy tests and her refusal to submit to complicated medical intervention, things got complicated and confusing, leaving them to wonder what the other was thinking and feeling.

They had to find a way back. It was still early in their marriage. They could mold their relationship into anything they needed it to be.

Christel was confident they would. It would simply take a lot of effort and some additional understanding on her part. He'd assured her that night that his absences were not intentional. She needed to push aside her trust issues and believe him.

Perhaps it was time to give in and take the infertility treatments. What would be the harm, really? She hated the idea, but if Evan wanted a baby so badly...who was she to turn from treating her inability to become pregnant?

She didn't need another failed marriage.

Christel ran harder, pounding the shade-dappled path with her feet...and her fractured thoughts.

At the break in the trees at the summit, she folded to the ground and took in the scenic panorama before her, letting the sun's rays warm her spirit. She'd made a decision, and it felt good to know there was a path forward.

Below, the lush and aromatic slope side was filled with Cook pine, eucalyptus, and tropical ash, creating a vista in shades of blue and green. A few feet from where Christal rested, palm grass and ginger sprouted at the base of wooden directional signs. She'd taken the west trail up the mountain and would follow the path down on the eastern side.

After a long swig of water, she screwed the cap back on and started her return run. Up ahead, she heard a dog bark in the distance.

Minutes later, a golden retriever appeared on the path heading her way. He charged her and jumped up, nearly knocking her over.

Laughing, she turned her face to avoid the dog's licks. "Are you alone?" she asked out loud. "Where's your master?"

Christel felt a presence and looked up.

Immediately, she couldn't breathe.

A man stood staring at her, a dog leash in his hand.

It was Jay.

23

Christel's heart pounded against her chest. "Jay?"

She stared again at her ex-husband, the man she hadn't seen in over two years. The man who cried and begged her not to go through with the divorce, who had promised he'd do better, be better.

The exchange nearly wrecked her as she signed the papers, her fingers trembling. He punched the attorney's office wall immediately after putting in a fist-sized hole that she paid to fix.

The man standing before her did not look like the same guy.

The hollow eyes were gone. The sunken cheeks and protruding bones in his face. The glassy look as he gazed at her. All were gone.

Instead, this man was reminiscent of the boy she'd fallen in love with in Chicago all those years before.

His brown hair was cut short. He was clean-shaven, and his amber eyes sparkled. His dimples appeared as he smiled at her.

Her ex-husband looked...sober?

"Jay?" she repeated.

Emotion flooded his face as he traversed the short distance between them. "Christel. It's good to see you." He tentatively pulled her into a light embrace and awkwardly let go. "Been a while."

"Yes," she agreed, unable to take her eyes from him. "You look..." she hesitated.

"Clean?" he offered.

He smiled again, and the dimples appeared. "I am. Nearly nineteen months...a whole year and a half of total sobriety." He rubbed at the back of his head, nervous. "I have you to thank for that."

She wasn't sure exactly how to respond, so she simply smiled back.

"Uh, you look good," he told her. "You've done something to your hair." He leaned and touched it. Then, as if remembering he no longer had the right to such intimacy, he quickly pulled back. "Looks nice."

He knelt and summoned his dog. "Come, Bacardi." He looked up at Christel as he clipped the leash back in place. "A bad joke."

Trying to act cool, she put in considerable effort to make her voice sound carefree. "What are you doing here?"

Jay lifted. "Well, you know that my dad left the island after Mom died. Took the insurance money and headed for Mexico. I was in Alaska when I got word he was in the hospital on a ventilator. Covid."

"Oh, no."

Jay thrust a hand deep inside his pocket. "Yeah, he didn't make it."

Given the rift between Jay and his father, Christel wasn't sure how to express her sympathy. The man was a horrible human being, and Jay hated him. "I'm...sorry."

He lifted his chin. "Yeah, don't be."

Christel nodded again. This time she looked away, not wanting Jay to see her examine him and the changes.

"Low and behold, the goat turd had property he never told us about...some rentals here on the island," Jay told her. "I'm here to settle some estate issues."

She nodded. "Oh, that makes sense." She wondered how long he would be on Maui but didn't ask.

Their eyes met, his gaze communicating he realized how hard this was for her. Jay understood her in a way few people did.

Finally, Jay shifted his feet. "Looks like you still like to run?"

"Yeah, I need the exercise, and it's peaceful up here."

"Looks like you have a ring on your finger," he pointed, his voice quiet yet stoic.

His words unexpectedly stabbed her in the heart. She never imagined standing here in front of the man she'd been madly in love with for so long...and having to admit she was now with someone else.

She'd moved on for good reason. Jay had abandoned her in more ways than one.

Yet, it was Jay who held her hand when she opened her bar exam results, who then retrieved the balloon bouquet from their bedroom that said 'Congratulations.' It was Jay who taught himself to cook rice and beans so she could study without stopping...the only food items they could afford while she was in school. It was Jay who dried her tears when storms grounded their plane, forcing them to be alone for Christmas and without her family. They'd spent that Christmas Eve walking along Navy Pier, holding hands and singing carols off-key while it was snowing. And, it was Jay who held her after making love for hours, who whispered tenderly against her ear, "I'll love you forever, you know."

Now, here he was, pointing at the ring on her hand—a ring that signified she now belonged to someone else.

"Yes," she admitted. Unexpected guilt weighed down on her. "His name is Evan."

"Evan Matisse. A doctor."

Christel frowned. "How did you—" She let her words fade.

Jay didn't answer. She noticed his hands trembling ever so lightly. His face looked pained as if he was working overtime to be okay with the situation when he was anything but.

Christel ached. "He's a good man," she told Jay. "He loves me."

He nodded, but not before Christel saw the moisture in his eyes. He lifted his hand and swept it away. "I'm clean, Christel. And I intend to stay that way."

At that moment, all the resentments faded. The horrible memories dimmed until she could no longer conjure a single one.

Her voice grew choked, feeling every ounce of the effort it took to seem normal. "I'm glad, Jay." As an afterthought, she felt the need to add, "I've always wanted the very best for you."

In a surprise move, Jay pulled her back into an embrace, clutching her tighter this time. "I love you, Christel," he whispered against her hair. "I always will."

He held her tight, and she let him. He smelled of the cologne she'd bought him his last birthday they'd spent together before it all started falling apart.

He touched her hand with his, lightly brushing his fingers against her skin before releasing her.

Jay drew a deep breath, releasing it slowly. Painfully. "Well, guess I should go. C'mon, Barcardi."

The dog danced at his feet, then followed as Jay took off jogging down the trail.

24

Christel's eyes immediately filled with tears. She blindly stumbled off the path until she came to a fallen tree trunk, where she sat, trying to breathe.

All the times she'd imagined seeing Jay again, nothing like what had just transpired ever came to mind. She'd especially never expected this level of emotion, this terrible ache.

Her kind, fractured, heartbroken Jay.

She thought she knew who she was, had her life down pat... and in moments, everything she believed about everything was turned upside down. Nothing made sense.

The realization of seeing Jay again washed over her like an ocean wave. Not one of those small waves that landed on the sand and slowly drifted to shore. No, this was the kind of set wave that swelled out of nowhere, the forceful kind that lifted you up on the water and toward the sun, carrying you whether or not you wanted to go.

A surge of loneliness came over her, settling deep and heavy in her heart. All she'd wanted to do was to sit with him, talk and hold his hand, tell him how she'd missed him.

So many questions remained. The gap between that day in

the attorney's office and today was just that...a gap. Where had he been? She'd heard he was working on a crabbing boat in Alaska. Was it there that he became sober? Did he go through yet another treatment program? What was it that worked this time? Certainly, her crying and begging had never been enough impetus for Jay to turn his life around.

She couldn't get over how good he looked. Healthy even. Like someone who ate granola and berries for breakfast—for dinner, quinoa topped with grilled salmon.

The idea of that brought a smile to her face. Jay loved Big Macs, fries, ice cream heavily drizzled with caramel sauce. The greasier and more sugar, the better.

Once, she chastised his eating habits, warning him his health was at risk. Jay had simply laughed before scooping her up and carrying her off to bed while singing:

"Two all-beef patties, special sauce, lettuce, cheese, pickles, onions, on a sesame seed bun."

He sang the McDonald's marketing tune off-key but with so much gusto it made her laugh as he laid her on the unmade bed and fell to the space beside her. In a matter of minutes, their clothes were on the floor and his mouth was on her skin.

"You don't play fair," she whispered with her eyes closed.

"And you think winning the game matters."

Christel felt a stab of regret.

Those early days after the divorce had nearly broken her. She wasn't sure where Jay ended and she began. The void was too big to conquer. She'd even kept one of his T-shirts in her drawer, pulling it out and sleeping with it.

Letting go of the hope that they would somehow return to *before*...well, it had left her heart forever fractured. Divorcing Jay was the hardest thing she'd ever done.

What choice did she have?

Jay's addiction made her feel like she was drowning. She left the marriage in order to keep from going under with him.

While she'd been forced into leaving, she'd never been able to exorcise him from her soul. You didn't pull glue apart that easily.

Christel turned suddenly nervous. She had no business letting this encounter with Jay unfold her. She was a divorced—and, more importantly—a remarried woman.

She loved Evan.

The fact was, she only loved the memory of Jay.

Armed with this renewed clarity, she sat up straight and fought to gain control of her emotions. She took a deep breath and stared into the distance for several minutes until her nerves were no longer stretched to the breaking point. Then, she stood, letting her eyes drift to the ring on her hand before she made her way back to the path.

With determination, Christel converted the mental battle into the distance beneath her feet remembering she was born with a warrior spirit.

She did what she knew to do.

She ran.

∽

Christel drove straight to her safe place...her mother's.

Her mom was out on her lanai when Christel arrived. Katie was with her. She could hear them laughing.

Christel pushed her sunglasses up on her head. "What's so funny?"

"Well, hey. There you are," Katie said. "I tried to call you."

Christel pulled her phone and saw the missed calls. "Sorry. I was on a hiking trail and didn't see the messages."

Katie grinned. "We're laughing about something Noelle said. She held up her sandwich and asked me to break it into three halves."

Christel joined them in laughing. Her niece was grower older by the minute...and cuter.

Their mother motioned for Christel to sit. She reached for the pitcher of iced tea. "Katie was telling me earlier that Aiden is having trouble with some girl."

Katie held her glass out for her mom to fill. "It's that girl Shane set him up with."

"Yeah, I heard. The one who got wasted and vomited on his feet."

Their mom stopped pouring. "Why do I not know of this?"

Both girls simply smiled.

Ava turned the pitcher and filled a glass for Christel. "C'mon...why am I always left in the dark?"

Christel shrugged. "All I know is what Shane told me over the phone. The girl showed up at the station acting as though she and Aiden were a thing. Awful pushy, if you ask me."

Katie agreed. "She doesn't sound anything like someone who Aiden would find attractive. I mean, Shane, maybe...but not Aiden."

Their mom put the tea pitcher back on the tray. "I hope he made his intentions clear. In both business and in romantic relationships, there is no room for mixed messages. You must be direct."

"I'm pretty sure he was, Mom. Problem was...she refused to accept what Aiden had to say. Apparently, she calls him several times a day. He finally had to block her."

Concern grew on Ava's face. "Well, I hope that ends the matter."

Christel nodded in agreement. "Yes, this is no time for Aiden to go all soft and refrain from hurting her feelings. He's going to have to put in a special order for some thicker skin and kick her to the curb."

A brief pause in their conversation followed...the break

Christel had been waiting for. She took a deep breath. "I saw Jay today."

Both women whipped their heads to face her.

"What?" Katie said. "You saw Jay?"

"Oh, honey," her mother muttered. "We all knew this day might come. How are you?"

Christel quickly teetered between reassuring them she was just fine and the truth. Opting for the former, she lifted her chin and lied. "It was nothing. Really."

She knew exactly what they were thinking. "He was sober," she said, reassuring them. "In fact, he looked really good. Like the old Jay."

A look crossed her mother's face...one of grave concern.

"What? Spit it out, Mom."

Her mother seemed to be trying to pick her words carefully. "He's...well, Jay has gotten sober before."

Katie nodded in agreement but said nothing.

Christel couldn't help it. She took offense.

She flashed her ring in the air. "Not my problem anymore. Remember?"

Her mom and Katie exchanged glances. Her mother quickly nodded. "Yes, yes...of course. You've moved on. Jay is sober and that's a good thing." She looked to her other daughter. "Right, Katie?"

Katie bobbed her chin up and down. "Right. A good thing."

25

Vanessa dropped Isabelle off for her first day at school, buoyed by the fact that she and her daughter had been getting along pretty well since the snorkeling trip. "Do you want me to go in with you? I can, if you think—"

"Got it," her daughter said, cutting her off.

Vanessa opened her mouth to argue—new schools could be unsettling—until she spotted Willa and Kina standing just inside the chain link fence. They waved at Isabelle, and a look of relief immediately filled her daughter's face. "Bye, Mom." She climbed from the car and jogged toward them with her backpack slung over her shoulder.

Isabelle seemed to acclimate to the new school well...that is, until Vanessa was pulled out of a strategy meeting a week later. "It's the school," Katie reported. "They said you aren't answering. You listed me as an emergency contact. They want you to come to the school as soon as possible."

Vanessa's heart went to her throat. "Is she okay?" She stood and grabbed her purse. "Is she sick?"

"I think she may have the attitude flu, if you know what I mean."

Vanessa's eyebrows lifted. "The what?"

"She's in the counselor's office."

The reality of the situation sunk in. "Ah...I see." Vanessa sighed, feeling her raised hopes suddenly dashed. "I'll be back as soon as I can."

"Take your time," Katie told her. "You can come to my house tonight, and I'll update you on how I think we need to approach the precinct chairman about getting out the vote." An unofficial poll showed Vanessa having a commanding lead, providing the voters not only registered but that they also showed up and cast their ballots at the voting booth on election day.

She could think about that later. "I'll call you," Vanessa told Katie. Right now, she needed to attend to Isabelle.

Less than half an hour later, she pulled into the school parking lot, got out of the car, and strode through the school to the counselor's office. At the closed door, she knocked sharply.

A muffled "come in" answered her.

Exhaling steadily, Vanessa collected herself and went inside.

The counselor, a pert brunette wearing pants made of flowing gauzy material and an oversized white blouse, smiled broadly and extended her hand. "Hello, Ms. Hart. I'm Nancy Berland. Please, come in."

Vanessa shook the woman's hand. "You can call me Vanessa."

Nancy took a seat behind her desk and pulled out a stack of papers. "Thank you for coming in so quickly."

Vanessa glanced around. "Where is Isabelle? What's the problem?"

"I asked you to come in because we're having some issues. I know it's only been a week, but Isabelle is simply sitting in the back of the classroom with her arms folded. Her teachers tell me they can tell she's bright, but she won't participate in discussions and has not turned in a single assignment." Nancy's face softened with sympathy. "And, today she left campus without permission. We were notified by our security officer, Harold. He saw her walking towards a waiting taxi. We thought we should alert you immediately."

Vanessa felt every word like a blow. She'd thought Isabelle was doing well, but it seemed her daughter was still angry and rebelling, and she didn't know what to do about it.

Nancy gazed steadily across the desk. "Would you like to talk about it?"

Vanessa quickly declined. Sure, she would love to have a lifeline here, to share her burden with this young woman, to lay her cards on the table and say, 'Help me, I'm lost here.'

She quickly reminded herself that she was running for state senator. She simply couldn't be that open. She'd have to do what she always did...buck up and be strong. Showing weakness was incomprehensible to her.

Right now, she needed to find her daughter.

"Thanks, but I'm good," she lied. "I'll talk to Isabelle. Get this turned around."

Vanessa stood. "Thank you for alerting me. My daughter is transitioning to a new place, a new school, and a whole new life, but she'll adjust." She paused, searching for how to end this dreadful conversation. "Given time."

Back in her car, Vanessa pulled her phone and quickly logged into the app, where she was able to track her daughter's new phone. In mere seconds, there was a ping and a red dot. The dot was stationary and no longer moving, so she must not still be traveling in the taxi.

Vanessa was worried Isabelle had somehow found the means to buy a ticket back to Seattle. Thankfully, the locator dot was not at the airport.

After texting Katie with an update, she headed for the address.

Minutes later, she pulled into the parking lot of the Maui Ocean Center Marine Institute. She grabbed her purse, exited her car, and headed for the entrance.

Behind the reception desk sat a balding man with thick coke-bottle glasses. "May I help you?" he asked.

"I'm looking for someone...my daughter," she explained.

Vanessa pulled out her wallet and withdrew a photograph. "Have you seen her?"

The man took the photo, leaned forward, and examined the image. He slowly shook his head.

"Are you sure?" Vanessa pressed, worried his eyesight might be hindered.

Just then, a woman appeared. She had black hair pulled into a bun at the nape of her neck and wore a pretty turquoise sleeveless dress. "Is there something I can help you with?" she offered.

Vanessa nodded. "My daughter. She's here, and I'm looking for her." She thrust the photo into the woman's hand.

"Ah, yes. Isabelle. She's out back."

"You know her?"

The woman smiled and nodded. "She's a lovely young woman. Isabelle comes here every day after school, or at least has for the past week."

Vanessa flinched at the new information. How had she not known? As usual, she'd barely noticed what was going on with her daughter.

The woman held out her hand. "I'm Inoa Opu'nui."

Vanessa shook her hand. "Vanessa Hart."

"Yes, you are running for state senator." The woman paused as if considering what she might say. "I'd love to talk to you sometime about the Institute and our work and the work of our foundation."

Oh, here it comes, Vanessa thought. A plug for funding.

She was wrong. Inoa simply smiled. "Let me take you to Isabelle."

They left the lobby and proceeded down a long hallway lined with posters of turtle rescues.

"Our team here at the Institute responds to reports, rescues, rehabilitates, and studies sea turtles on the island of Maui, Hawaii. We employ staff biologists, but most of our essential work is carried on by dedicated volunteers...like Isabelle."

Before Vanessa could respond to that surprising news, they moved through a door and into what appeared to be a laboratory lined with metal tables and cabinets. Two men hovered over a turtle on the far side of the room. Isabelle stood close by with an instrument in her hand, ready to pass it off when the men were ready for it.

Vanessa was taken aback. "Isabelle?"

Her daughter turned, and immediately apprehension filled her features. "Mom, I can explain."

26

Aiden lifted the hammer, drove a nail into a two-by-four, and then stepped back to survey his work.

Despite spending most of his free time working on home renovations, the small thirteen-hundred-square-foot single-story in Lahaina a couple of years back still needed a lot of work.

He'd spent the first year tearing up moldy orange shag carpet and pulling down wood paneling from the walls. His parents thought he was nuts.

Before he passed, his dad warned, "The electrical is outdated, son. Looks dangerous."

His mother had nodded in agreement. "Honey, I want to be happy for you. Really, I do. I'm afraid this place will be nothing more than a money pit. Come home," she urged. "Move back to Pali Maui and save some money toward a bigger down payment. When it's time, we'll help you out when you find something...nicer. We'll lend financial support." She'd looked to his dad. "In fact, we could do that now, couldn't we, Lincoln?"

Since his promotion to captain at the Maui Emergency Management Services, Aiden could shoulder the renovation costs much easier. No longer was upgrading this old house a financial burden.

The first room he completed was the kitchen. His sister, Katie, had worked with a world-class architect to build her home at Pali Maui, and she was more than generous with her advice. At times, too much.

But what did he know about house design?

After a bit of negotiation—Katie's taste far exceeded his budget—they'd gone with something reasonably simple. While the room was an odd size and required custom cabinets, he'd been able to secure discounted granite for the countertops and went to the local home building goods store for the hardware, a sink, and faucets. He'd also purchased mid-level appliances. Nothing fancy. But nice.

He'd gone with a neutral light gray for the wall color and painted the entire house the same shade. "That makes your living space and all the rooms look bigger," Katie advised.

The flooring was next. That little project required him to move out for about a week. He'd stayed with his mom while engineered wood floors were installed. Windows came next. Those had to be custom as well.

With the big projects crossed off his list, he was now installing molding before he took the big plunge and turned over his furnishing budget to Katie. "That's it," he warned. "Don't go over."

"I am fully capable of staying within financial confines," she told him. "Ask Aunt Vanessa. She trusts me with the campaign budget, and I haven't let her down. Just the opposite." She leaned forward and grinned. "Come to find out; I am a shrewd negotiator when it comes to pricing."

Aiden now rubbed at the back of his neck. He was short a couple of board feet, meaning he'd have to make a trip to the building supply store.

As he headed for the door, he chastised himself for not

measuring correctly. He knew he should have measured twice and cut once.

After locking the door, he headed down the sidewalk and for his jeep.

That's when he noticed a slip of white paper positioned under the windshield wiper. Aiden scowled and pulled it out, unfolded the paper.

Hey, Aiden. I haven't heard from you since that day at the station. I feared you might have lost my number. My cell is 808-347-3900. Call anytime. Day or night. I'll be waiting. ~Sydney

Aiden stared at the words on the note, growing increasingly confused. Had he given any indication he would call? Not that he remembered. He didn't want to see her again. He'd hoped his lack of attention might send that message.

The thought hit him that she knew where he lived. He made a mental note to ask Shane not to share his private information. This was a girl he truly just wanted to distance himself from.

He folded the paper and moved to the driver's side, then slid into the seat of his doorless jeep. Leaning, he opened the glovebox and tossed the note inside, closing the compartment door with a deep frown as he thought of Sydney.

By all accounts, he was a gentleman and never intentionally hurt anyone's feelings. Yet, the old saying was indeed true.

Some people walk into your life and leave footprints on your heart. Others walk into your life, and all you want is to leave footprints on their face!

27

Evan wolf-whistled when Christel walked into the bedroom wearing a silk camisole in a pretty blush color with matching panties, a color she knew highlighted her blonde hair and blue eyes. "Hot mama," he muttered, reaching for her.

Christel once read that every marital rift could be resolved with a good romp in bed. She had no data, no published studies to back up the assertion, but from anecdotal evidence, she wouldn't dispute the claim.

On the dresser were chocolate-dipped strawberries and an ice bucket with champagne. She'd even bought a large bouquet of flowers, just to make things extra special.

Evan ran his fingers along her chin. "I thought we were supposed to go to that fundraiser tonight."

Christel simply smiled and slowly shook her head in the negative. "Change of plans."

Evan grinned and quickly unbuttoned his dress shirt. "How'd you pull that off?"

"I told Aunt Vanessa and Katie we were celebrating having a

night alone together." She didn't remind him that it had been well over two weeks since they'd gone to bed at the same time.

She also didn't add that she'd run into Jay. She knew she should. First, she'd have to find the words because, for the life of her, she couldn't seem to form any.

The incident was still too fresh. Too fragile. She didn't know how to make sense of it yet. Or of her feelings.

Evan kissed her, and she relaxed into his arms. Being with him felt like kicking off a pair of heels after a long day at work. Natural, freeing, effortless.

"I love you," he said as he slid his hand under her camisole top.

She warmed to his touch and let her fingers roam across his bare chest before dropping to his belt.

And those beautiful flowers ended up scattered all over the floor.

~

HOURS LATER, Christel woke up in the middle of the night feeling panicked. Her forehead broke into a sweat, and her chest squeezed against the pounding of her heart.

In the dark, her mind saw Jay standing on the trail, looking at her with that smile she'd seen a thousand times. The one that showed off his dimples and made her grow warm inside.

She heard his voice. "I'm clean, Christel. And I intend to stay that way."

She squeezed her eyes shut, still remembering how he bent and rubbed his dog's fur before standing and pulling her against him, so close she felt his heart beat against her own racing heart—heard his quiet proclamation, "I love you, Christel. I always will."

Two years had passed since she was Jay's wife. Love had many meanings, and his declaration had no doubt been simply one of familial affection. What he'd whispered against her ear didn't necessarily mean he was *in love* with her.

Even so, Christel's instinct was to grab Jay tightly, to put her hand over his mouth in order to stop him from saying all of that.

What did it matter?

She was not still in love with Jay. Her middle-of-the-night thoughts were racing because there were so many unanswered questions. So many gaps.

Where had he been and what had he been through in these past two years?

The unknown had been grueling and left her imagining all kinds of scenarios. She'd been afraid the disease would kill him. No one knew she quietly waited for "the call." Even after the divorce.

Then, there he was. Sober and smiling at her.

For years, Jay was her best friend. Her confidante. They shared everything. Nothing was hidden between the two of them...at least before the drinking began. That was perhaps the hardest adjustment of all...the loss of her companion, her mentor, her counselor. That kind of intimacy was hard to replicate.

Despite his addiction, the good memories of him were still inside her, protected and cared for.

That didn't mean she and Evan were not close. He adored her, no question. She loved him deeply. Evan was her safe place —her refuge after the storm of Jay.

Christel lay in the dark and tried to settle her breathing.

In...out. In...out. That's it.

Somehow, being in touch with Jay seemed dangerous. She still hadn't untangled the knot of emotions, hadn't teased out how she truly felt about seeing him again.

Perhaps this answered why she hadn't told Evan yet.

Evan would ask hard questions, she knew. How could she

put into words and convey to her husband what she couldn't form in her own head?

One thing she was sure of. Most couples divorced because they had grown to hate one another. Despite what he'd put her through, she could never hate Jay.

28

Vanessa pulled into the drop-off line at Isabelle's school, trying to hide her annoyance at the long length of cars. Juggling this mothering thing with running a high-profile campaign was more than a little arduous. She made a mental note to tell Katie to maneuver this issue into her platform. A promise to address this issue would surely garner votes from mothers.

"Do you have everything, honey?" she asked, looking across the seat at her daughter.

Isabelle nodded. "You're going to pick me up after school and drive me to the rescue center, right?"

Vanessa nodded. "And you agree to keep our bargain? You participate in class, and I play after-school chauffeur." She eased her car up in the line.

"You got it."

Vanessa took the opportunity to start a conversation. "So, tell me about this gal who runs the Marine Institute?"

"Iona?"

"Yes, she seemed nice." Vanessa's phone buzzed. Hoping it

was nothing critical, she remained focused on her daughter. "Do you like her?"

"Oh, yes," Isabelle confessed. "Iona is good friends with Halia Aka, Kina's mom. They live together at the Banana Patch."

The Banana Patch was a women's wellness retreat center here on the island. A little boho hippy for her taste, but she'd met Halia, and she was a lovely woman. Moreover, Willa and Kina had sidled up to her daughter and became instant friends. Even at sixteen, it had to be hard to walk into a school and not know anyone. Willa and Kina had eliminated that issue for Isabelle.

Isabelle dropped the visor down and examined her reflection in the tiny mirror, then slapped it back in place. "Iona says my interest in Hono is extraordinary. Did you know that when sea turtles first hatch, they are omnivores and eat anything they catch? Once they're about the size of a dinner plate, they turn almost exclusively vegetarian, feeding primarily on nine different types of algae." Her face broke into a wide grin. "Yet, they'll still occasionally enjoy a snack of passing jellyfish."

"Wow. Interesting."

Vanessa's phone buzzed again. It was everything in her not to pick it up. She was ready to give in and answer when Isabelle looked over and said, "Mom. Inoa thinks I could be a marine biologist. She says she could get me a student internship at the Marine Institute and help me land some scholarships. With her recommendation and that of the board members, she tells me I would be assured a spot in the coveted program at the University of Hawaii."

That piqued Vanessa's attention. "That means you'd stay?" she nearly whispered.

"Can you believe it?" Isabelle said with her hand on the door handle as they inched forward. "I can get out here." She opened the door and scrambled out. Before shutting the door, she peered back at her mother. "Don't forget to pick me up. And don't be late." She slammed the door closed, hiked her backpack on her shoulder, and headed toward where Willa and Kina stood waiting.

Vanessa immediately pulled out her phone and scanned the incoming messages. Nothing critical, thank goodness. Her thumbs flashed across the tiny screen as she typed out a text to Katie asking her to address some of the issues raised in the incoming messages.

Honk!

Vanessa glanced in the rearview mirror and frowned. She'd love to shake a fist at the impatient offender. Knowing her luck, someone would catch her action on their camera, and the image would show up all over the internet.

VANESSA HEADED for the door into her campaign office, buoyed with the idea that Isabelle was not only acclimating to living here with her but had nearly said she planned to stay. Vanessa let the notion that her daughter would remain after graduation and likely make Maui her home as she started her new life...as a marine biologist. The thought both warmed and excited Vanessa, and she couldn't hide her happiness.

"What's up with you?" Katie asked as Vanessa entered the office. "You look like you just got handed a chocolate-covered ice cream cone on a hot day." Her eyes widened. "You got word we landed the endorsement from Bill from the hotel association? His donation came in yesterday." She grinned. "Very generous, I might add."

Vanessa shook her head. "No endorsement yet, but I have something even better. I think Isabelle is going to stay."

"Here? With you?"

"Yes, with me."

Vanessa shook off the notion. Katie was so surprised. Her mental reservations did not mean everyone else had a license to question whether she could pull off this mothering thing. She'd always been able to accomplish anything she'd set her mind to. Her mind was set on convincing Isabelle to stay. Her mind was set on blazing a relationship with her daughter, becoming friends even. Her mind was set on showing Clark she was a better parent than he ever gave her credit for being. She'd block him from creating any further wedge between her and Isabelle.

Her mind raced far ahead to the day she'd be the one helping Isabelle choose a wedding gown. She would be the one by her daughter's bedside when she welcomed their grandchild. She would spend holidays and birthdays and have lunch dates with her daughter. Someday, they would be best friends.

"I have Willa to thank."

Katie scooped up a stack of campaign door knockers and placed them on a shelf next to cellophane-wrapped glossy mailers. "My Willa?"

"Yes. Willa and her best friend, Kina, have scooped up Isabelle and included her in their circle of friends. Kina's mother introduced her to a woman named Inoa, who lives with them at the Banana Patch. Inoa works at the Maui Ocean Center Marine Institute in Wailuku."

"Oh, yes. I know Inoa. She's great."

"She's more than great. She's convinced Isabelle she can stay on the islands and attend the University of Hawaii to become a marine biologist."

Katie beamed. "That's wonderful."

A commotion at the door drew both of the women's attention. In walked a man wearing a pair of khaki chinos and a button-down short-sleeved black shirt with a tropical decal embroidered onto the front pocket. "I hope I'm not barging in," he said.

"Bill, of course not." Vanessa quickly moved to greet him. They shook hands. "What brings you to see us?" She exchanged excited glances with Katie.

He let out a loud laugh. "Well, let's cut to the chase, shall we? Your campaign team has been courting my endorsement for a couple of weeks. I'm here to extend that endorsement."

Before she could thank him, he quickly added, "Providing we have that agreement I mentioned at the fundraiser the other evening. We need your help as well."

"The hotel association is high on my list of priorities," Vanessa promised. "Tourism factors in as one of the top influencers of the island's economy." She reached, and they shook.

Katie couldn't help but clap her hands together.

"Now, I'd like to take you two ladies out to lunch with a couple of friends," he said. "And I won't take no for an answer."

Lunch was at Kapa Grill, located inside the Marriott. They were joined by the manager of the hotel as well as half a dozen other members of the hotel industry. Over a specially made entrée of seafood fettuccine, which included a generous topping of mussels, shrimp, scallops, and crab meat mixed in a creamy lobster sauce, they discussed their concerns and what they hoped the state legislature might do to help.

The martinis were flowing, and so were the demands. Endorsements were not free.

Vanessa learned that the hotel folks had recently formed a PAC, a political action committee, to unite and fight legislation that threatened their profits. The PAC was heavily funded by local lodging establishments and national franchises that had a massive stake in the island's hospitality industry.

"We're not asking for much," Bill said, ordering yet another martini. "We're only hoping for policies that create a fair business environment, allowing the lodging industry to create jobs and grow Maui's economy."

Vanessa knew that was quiet speak for letting her know the

recent pandemic had dished their industry a significant hit. They couldn't afford to be generous and give in to pressures from interests that opposed their own.

Vanessa leaned across the table. Her one martini remained half-full as she determined to stay focused. "Gentlemen, I am a candidate who will work to balance marine protections as well as back our island's hoteliers who have remained resilient under incredible recent burdens. If elected, you can count on me to help you be optimistic about the future."

Her charm and razor-sharp ability to narrow in on what they cared about and address their concerns won them over. Before the lunch ended, not only did she have the endorsement, but a generous donation from the PAC and several of them individually.

"I, for one, believe we have found our candidate. You have our full support," promised one hotel manager as he pulled out his checkbook and pen.

On the short walk back to the campaign office, Katie was giddy. "I can't believe you pulled that off," she exclaimed.

"We pulled that off," Vanessa clarified. "It takes a team. You are an incredible asset to that effort." She drew her niece into a hug. "We're on our way. This is going to be the race to watch on election night. I feel in my bones that we're going to land on top. And, I rarely miss."

They were only feet from the office door when Katie's expression changed, and she grew worried. "One question, Aunt Vanessa. What will you do when Isabelle learns you are supporting the hotel PAC who is the main player fighting the conservation efforts to save the Hono in those delicate bays near the hotels?"

Vanessa suddenly stopped walking. For someone who rarely missed, she'd let that one slide entirely over her head. She blamed the excitement over the much-needed support.

"I'm not sure," she said with determination. "But I'll find a way to make everyone happy. That's politics."

Suddenly, she glanced down at her watch. "Oh my gosh! What time is it?"

Without waiting for an answer, she turned and ran toward the parking garage.

"Where are you going?" Katie shouted after her.

"To pick up my daughter at school!"

29

Shane pulled Carson from his car seat and headed for his brother's front door. Aiden had been working on house renovations and claimed he was nearly finished. "Come take a look," he'd offered. "I'm anxious for you guys to see how the changes turned out."

So, Shane decided to take him up on it. Especially when Aiden told him he'd also invited Katie and Christel. His siblings tried to connect regularly by meeting for lunch at Charley's in Pa'ia. Lately, they'd all grown so busy that many weeks had passed without getting to hang out.

Shane lifted Carson onto his hip and reached inside the car for the diaper bag. Katie's car pulled up behind his, and she cut the engine. When she stepped from the car, Carson wiggled wildly as he recognized his aunt. As she neared, he held out tiny chubby hands in her direction.

"Well, hey, little guy!" She pulled him from Shane's arms and hugged the little guy. "You keeping your daddy out of trouble?"

"Is that even possible?" Aiden said as he strode down the sidewalk toward them.

"Hey, no throwing shade." Shane greeted this brother with a fist bump.

"I owe you," Aiden told him as he moved to join Katie. He grabbed his nephew's head and planted a big uncle kiss on top.

The baby giggled and said, "Daden."

Aiden's hand went to his chest. "Oh, my goodness. Did Carson just say my name?"

Both Shane and Katie nodded. "It appears so," Katie confirmed.

"Give me that boy!" Aiden lifted the tiny toddler from Katie's arms. "You want your uncle to buy you a car? How about a Hummer open-top? Nothing is too good for my nephew."

Aiden headed back for the house and waved for his siblings to follow. "Where's Christel? She's normally the first one to arrive anywhere."

Katie placed her hand on her brother's back. "There's a story there. Let's take a tour, and then we'll sit down, and I'll get you both up to date on all things Christel."

Shane's brows lifted. "She's not coming?"

Katie confirmed that was the case. "She claims she's exhausted after being up all night. She might join us later, but said not to worry if she doesn't show."

"Dang. It's getting harder and harder to get us all together." Aiden pulled the fridge door open. "Want something to drink?"

"A beer," Shane said.

"Me, too." Katie grinned at her nephew. "And some cheerios for this little guy."

"Got it covered." Shane pulled a Ziploc of baby treats from the diaper bag and pulled his son from his sister's arms. "He loves these little banana-flavored puffs." He got his little boy settled up to the counter using a trick their mom had taught and secured Carson into the bar stool by tying a kitchen towel around him. Shane checked to ensure the baby couldn't fall and then placed the treats before him.

Carson immediately reached and put one of the puffs in his mouth and smiled back at his daddy.

When Carson had finished eating, Shane unfastened his son and picked him up. "Okay, let's see this house."

Aiden took his siblings for a tour, showing them all the renovations. He showed them the flooring, the molding, the kitchen cabinets, and the pantry remodel. They ooh'd and ah'd over the bathroom shower with the doorless entry and hardware that created a rain shower effect.

"I love the tile," Katie exclaimed.

Shane nodded with pride. "You should. You picked it out."

"Which is why I like it so much."

When the tour was over, they made their way back into the living room, and Aiden got them another round of beers.

Katie pointed to Carson. "He's out."

Shane placed him on the sofa next to him with his hand on his stomach to ensure he didn't roll off.

Aiden shook his head. "Bro, I'll never get over seeing you like this. Who would've thought you'd be a nominee for Dad of the Year?"

Shane shook his head and grinned. "Nothing compares, dude. Besides, I'd like to meet the liar who says his life turned out exactly as planned."

Aiden held up his hands. "Well, despite your passing out my personal information to every stalker in town, I think I'll hold off for a while."

Katie pulled her legs up crosswise on the sofa. "Yeah, how's that going? The girl, I mean?"

Shane shook his head. "Yeah, hey. I'm sorry. Who could've seen that coming? I mean, apparently, I don't have a great nose for picking up on psycho women." He pointed his thumb at Carson.

Katie lifted her can of beer in triumph. "Well, finally. You figured that out."

Shane rolled his eyes before turning to Aiden. "So, if Sydney is still bothering you—shake her off already."

"Bro, I tried. How many times do I have to claim to be too busy to see her before she gets the message? How many unanswered phone calls and unreturned messages before she clues in that I'm not interested?"

"Send her a text and blow her off," Shane suggested.

"You think I haven't tried that?"

Katie sighed. "Oh, you guys." She looked at Aiden as if he were a child. "Just call her and say, 'Leave me alone. I'm not interested.'"

Aiden visibly shuddered. "Uh, I'm not sure I want to actually talk to her," he teased. "That sounds a little too direct."

Katie downed her beer, then looked over at her sleeping nephew. "My brothers are both socially inept. You know that?"

In response, Aiden threw a sofa pillow at her.

"Okay, be that way. But I have news. News I don't necessarily have to share with my brothers."

They both immediately leaned forward with their full attention. "What news?" they said in unison.

Katie laughed. "You two are like two gossipy old women."

"Enough with the editorial. Just spill already," Aiden urged. "What do you know? Is it about Mom and Tom? Or, I know...is Mig giving in and marrying Wimberly Ann?"

"Is she pushing for that?" Shane asked.

"Oh, will you two please focus? I have news about Christel."

Her brothers exchanged glances.

"What about Christel?" Shane asked.

Katie leaned forward. "Jay's back."

"What? What do you mean Jay's back?" Aiden asked, setting his beer can on the coffee table. "How do you know that?"

"She ran into him on Kahakapao while going for a run."

Shane scowled. "Sounds like more than a coincidence."

"I don't know about that, but she claims he's sober."

"We've heard that before," Aiden said. "I mean, I like Jay and all. But Christel went through a lot. I don't want her getting sucked back into his mess."

Shane scowled again. "She's married," he said as if that fact solved the problem.

Aiden straightened and laughed softly. "You think that'll matter? Jay is Christel's soft spot."

Shane doubled a fist and slammed it into the sofa cushion. "We have to protect her."

"Really? And how do you propose to do that?" Katie asked.

"I don't know...yet," he said. "But Christel deserves to be happy."

Aiden leaned back into the sofa cushions and wishboned his arms behind his head. "We'll find a way."

30

Isabelle's bedroom door slammed.

Vanessa's skin prickled with regret. Such a powerful word, seeped in failure she felt helpless to fix.

No matter how many times Vanessa had apologized to her daughter for neglecting to pick her up on time, the ride home had been met with folded arms and absolute silence.

Vanessa had always considered herself a master at juggling balls in the air, but lately, she'd been dropping some important ones. What was a woman to do when two equally important things pulled at her in two different directions?

Bill and the others from the hotel association expected her full attention in order to come through with their support for her election. Her daughter was counting on her promise to pick her up and take her to the marine rescue center.

How could she simply blow either of them off?

In the end, Vanessa let both of them down.

She pulled a bottle of chilled Reisling from the refrigerator and poured herself an ample glass. She took a sip, feeling the tension build between her shoulder blades.

Her life was like a rubber band being pulled to the breaking point. One more tug and the big snap would occur.

Oh, sure...she could swoop in and smooth over the issues with her potential constituents. All she had to do was promise them the moon. She didn't even want to consider that the moon was in exact opposition to the turtles that meant so much to Isabelle.

Despite her resolve, she was letting her daughter down again. She needed to do damage control.

She carried her stemmed glass down the hallway and stopped in front of her daughter's bedroom door. She rapped lightly. "Isabelle?"

No answer.

Not put off, Vanessa slipped her hand onto the knob and turned it. She pushed the door open slightly. "Honey?"

Inside, her daughter lay face down on her unmade bed.

Vanessa sat down beside her. "Isabelle, listen to me. I know people say the teen years are hard, but it's far worse being a grownup. You climb on board the carousel hoping to never betray your intentions, to never let anyone down. The damn thing never stops turning. The demands whiz by and it seems you can never get off."

Her daughter lifted her head from the crumpled pillow. "That's what you have to say? Life isn't a carnival, Mom. I'm not some prize you collect for winning."

"What do you mean?"

"I'm your daughter."

Vanessa frowned. "I know that."

"Do you? Have you ever for one moment stepped into my shoes and considered what it was like to be your daughter?"

Vanessa opened her mouth to reply but Isabelle sat up and raised her hands in mock surrender. "Don't. You don't have to keep trying so hard. I know how it is...how it's always been."

Despite her anger, Isabelle's eyes pooled with moisture. She jumped up and moved to the top drawer of her dresser and pulled out what appeared to be a handmade book. Isabelle tossed it into Vanessa's lap.

Puzzled, Vanessa lifted the well-worn stapled object and inspected the cover with a rudimentary stick-figure image of a hand-drawn woman holding a little girl's hand. Without comment, she turned the cover. Inside were colored drawings and child-like printed words.

The story was of a little girl who was having a birthday party. She was surrounded by presents…and the mom.

On the following page, the story continued. That same little girl appeared to be on a backyard swing. Her mother pushed her high into the sky with a single carefully printed word underneath. "Whee!"

Next came a scene with a castle with tall spires and a black mouse with oversized ears. The same little girl and mother stood in front. The little girl's exaggerated red smile nearly covered her face.

"What is this?" Vanessa asked.

Isabelle lifted her chin and said nothing. Instead, she picked at a loose thread on a wadded pair of jeans she'd thrown onto the top of her bed.

"Is this you, and me?"

Isabelle nodded.

Her daughter's quivering chin pierced her heart. Her own eyes filled with tears as her mind filled with each of the incidents—the missed birthday party…perhaps more than one, the times she was too busy to play because her briefcase was packed with research notes that needed read before the morning show, the trip to Disneyworld they had to cancel because she was on a big story in the newsroom.

The reality of the loss seen through her daughter's eyes made her throat nearly close with emotion.

She swallowed and took Isabelle's young teenage hands

into her own. "Oh, honey. I'm so...sorry. Please believe me. I love you, sweetheart. All of the good parts of me are because of you, Isabelle."

Sixteen years ago, when the nurse had handed that tightly wrapped bundle into her arms, Vanessa had vowed to herself to protect Isabelle from the world, to ensure nothing ever hurt her. In the end, it was Vanessa herself who had been the biggest threat to her daughter's happiness.

At that moment, she made a decision.

She knew the consequences. She knew what it would cost her.

She was going to do it anyway.

31

Aiden lifted the Starbucks coffee container to his mouth, drained the last of his Espresso Macchiato, and then tossed the empty cup into the industrial-sized trash receptacle just inside the station door.

A television mounted on a wall to the left of the door leading to the kitchen blared with an announcement. "Breaking news!"

Aiden frowned and joined Jeremy Hogan, who stood listening with his hands on his hips. Breaking news always garnered rapt attention from the rescue crew in the station.

A voiceover rang out atop an image of the entrance to his aunt's campaign office. "This morning, candidate for Hawaii state senator Vanessa Hart pulled out of the race citing personal reasons."

The camera panned to Vanessa, who stood stoic in a suit and heels, wearing a smile. "I've already talked to my primary opponent, Jim Kahale. My entire staff will join his and make a run to serve the great state of Hawaii in all the ways that matter most to the people I intended to serve." When asked what prompted her decision, she simply smiled. "I have a job that is far more important. Everything else must be squeezed in around that priority."

Aiden shook his head. His Aunt Vanessa was nothing if not filled with surprises.

"Hey, bro. Looks like you have a visitor." Jeremy nodded in the direction of the door.

A woman with a familiar face stood, hands on hips and a camera dangling from a strap around her neck. Without missing a beat, she marched forward and smiled. "Well, he does still exist," she stated.

Like mice faced with the presence of a cat, his buddies quickly scattered, leaving him alone with Sydney Alexander, who was fast becoming his least favorite person.

"Hey," Aiden said, which was all he could muster.

"Thought I'd let you know that I've arranged to stay on the island indefinitely. Starly is going to let me stay with her." She lifted the camera. "The shots here are amazing. I've licensed and sold several images already."

Aiden felt his insides tighten. That's all he needed.

"So, I thought maybe we could see more of each other?" she suggested. "I mean, I really feel like we have a connection." She fingered the buttons on her blouse. "What do you say you come over tonight for a few drinks?"

"Uh, I—I can't," Aiden muttered. "Lots to do. Paperwork stacked up to here." He motioned with a hand above the level of his head.

She waved off his protests. "Oh, pooh. You can do that later. You're the captain. What are you going to do? Fire yourself?"

Aiden shook his head. "Doesn't work like that."

Sydney moved closer.

Aiden stepped back.

She closed the space between them, then lifted a hand and let her finger trace the line of his chin. "I'd make it very worth your while."

His stomach sank. She could keep her suggested favors. Nothing sounded bleaker than spending time with this girl.

Suddenly, Aiden felt a hand on his shoulder. He turned to find Megan McCord.

His co-worker drew a deep breath. "Sorry, apparently you didn't get the message. Aiden Briscoe is taken."

Before he could let her words sink in, she pulled him to herself. Without another word, she took his face in her hands and tilted his face to meet her own, pressing her mouth against his.

Her mouth fit his perfectly. It started soft and gentle, then the kiss deepened, turned wrenching and dangerous. Her tongue slipped into his mouth.

Aiden couldn't help but respond. Everything faded as he gave himself over to that kiss. As if on autopilot, his hand reached and cupped her chin. He kissed her back, hard and deep.

Without warning, the kiss ended.

Megan stepped back and drilled Sydney with a look that could turn a burning tree to ice. "Any questions?"

Sydney stumbled back. "Uh, no." She lifted her hands in mock surrender. "I didn't know."

Meegan looped her hand in the hook of Aiden's arm, stifling a grin. "Don't you have somewhere to be?"

Sydney stared at the tiger tattoo on Megan's arm, and her expression turned to stone. "Look, all he had to do was say so."

Megan made a sweeping motion with her hand, directing the unwanted girl to be gone.

Sydney quickly obeyed. She turned without a word and headed for the door.

When she was gone, Aiden stood transfixed, still reeling from that kiss.

What had just happened?

Megan's face broke into a wide grin. "You're welcome," she

said. Then, leaning forward, "You'd better not file a harassment claim."

Dumbfounded, Aiden shook his head. "Uh, no. I won't."

Megan laughed, patted him on the butt, and headed for the kitchen.

32

Nearly a week had passed since Christel had run into Jay on the hiking trail. A long seven days of fighting to turn off the thoughts that raged inside, especially in the middle of the night when sleep eluded her.

Jay had been her first—and her only—boyfriend for many years. They'd met briefly at a beach party the summer before she'd graduated from high school. He walked straight up to her, smiled, and said, "Hey, you look a little lost. Okay if I get you a beer?"

She passed on the beer but did join him on a piece of koa wood that had drifted up on the beach. They sat and chatted for hours. He ended up asking her out, but she declined.

Several years later, she was working as a volunteer at a local election office, helping to register voters when a familiar-looking guy wearing jeans and a casual white button-down showed up at the campaign office. He had brown hair tossed boyishly around his face and nearly laughed with amusement as his eyes scanned the room.

The minute he saw her he smiled. When he did, deep

dimples formed. He sauntered over. "Hey, you look a little lost. Okay if I get you a beer?" he asked, looking as if he had just unilaterally won the biggest campaign of all.

So much of them fit together perfectly back then. Despite her high-strung nature and his laid-back approach to life, he seemed to fill her empty places. When she worried, he sat her on the sofa and told her knock-knock jokes while rubbing her feet.

He taught her to cook without a recipe. "Measuring takes all the fun out," he said. "Go with your gut. You have a great gut." He lifted her shirt, bent, and kissed her stomach.

He knew her cautious side and urged her toward adventure, even taking her skydiving. They jumped out together holding hands. She had never felt that free-spirited in her entire life. Nor since.

Jay once woke her in the middle of the night and led her into a candlelit bathroom with a tub filled with scented water and petals floating on the surface. She leaned against him for hours while he washed her hair and sang Fleetwood Mac songs.

When they made love, he knew she often became overwhelmed with emotion and quietly kissed away tears at the corners of her eyes as their bodies came together.

Those early memories filled Christel's mind. In the darkness, she'd reach for Evan and fold herself to him as if to reassure herself that she had the power to disarm them. Yet, no matter how hard she tried, she couldn't seem to chase them away.

Something told her Jay was awake and thinking of her as well.

So, when he texted her the following day, Christel was not all that surprised.

"*Christel, you can say no but I want to see you. One of the facets* of my rehabilitation program is to make amends. I've formed conversations in my head a thousand times, telling you how sorry I am for what I put you through. I feel I owe it to you to tell you in person. Would you be willing to meet me and talk?"

Christel stared at her phone for what seemed like an eternity before her shaking fingers moved to the screen and she typed out a reply.

"I don't think that's a good idea."

She swallowed and pushed send, immediately filled with regret. The quick and short response no doubt hurt him. She had no reason, nor did she wish, to make him feel bad. They were two grown people who had once meant everything to each other. Circumstances had pulled them apart and they were now on different journeys. What harm could there be in simply meeting and talking?

She quickly typed another reply.

"On second thought, sure...I'd like that. I have a lot of questions."

Christel could imagine him smiling as he read that. He knew she loved information and hated to be in the dark about anything.

She waited.

Finally, her phone dinged.

"Great!"

They arranged to meet at Hanakao'o Beach Park with plans to walk the Ka'anapali Trail, a three-mile stretch of cement boardwalk following the edge of the ocean and passing by several of the island's large destination resorts. The pathway was the perfect blend of public and private, better than meeting alone at his house, or in a noisy restaurant where it would be difficult to talk.

Christel pulled into the nearly empty parking lot at exactly four o'clock in the afternoon, their agreed-upon time. At first, she believed she was the first to arrive but soon spotted Jay sitting alone at a picnic table mounted on a pad of concrete. He saw her as well and waved.

Her legs tingled as she climbed from her car, the way they always did before a big test in college. She took a deep breath and headed his way.

Their eyes met as she neared. Jay stood and leaned into her, swept a light kiss on her cheek. "I'm glad you agreed to meet me," he told her.

"Me, too."

"Do you want to walk?" he pointed north in the direction of the Hyatt Regency. In the distance, the ocean's surface shimmered beyond a row of canoes lining the shore. Palm fronds swayed in the gentle breeze.

She nodded, feeling a sense of peace wash over her. There was nothing to be nervous about. This was Jay...her Jay. The fact that they hadn't spoken in two years only meant they had a lot to catch up on.

"Does Evan know you are here?" he asked, immediately putting her guard back up.

For a moment she considered lying. Why disclose what she knew he would want explained?

He slowed and gazed at her. There was no hiding...there never had been.

"No," she said, guilt weighing on her.

Jay simply nodded.

"Well, as I said, I'm grateful you granted me this opportunity. There is a lot I need to say."

Christel shook her head. "You don't really need to apologize..."

He boldly took her hand. "Yes, I do."

They walked past the old cemetery and the crumbling headstones with rudimentary markings in Japanese script. Tufts of grass bordered the stones as if they'd been left unattended too long.

"I'm the one who killed our marriage," Jay said. "I know you well enough to know you blame yourself, even if in some small manner. But nothing about what happened to us was your fault. Nothing."

Christel felt a familiar constriction in her throat.

"I spent a lot of time in counseling. I now understand how powerless I was over my addiction and why the drinking had such control over me."

He explained how he had explored the relationship with his father and his early childhood, and how painful it had been to never be loved or praised as a young boy. "There was always something missing," Jay confessed. "When you came along... well, it was the best thing that ever happened to me. Unfortunately, my love for you was never enough to overcome the demons I wrestled deep within."

"And now?" Christel asked, so aware of the feel of his fingers entwined in her own, it hurt.

"I'm coming to terms with myself." Jay rubbed at his cheek. "Addicts deny that we're tired, we deny that we're scared, we deny how badly we want to succeed. And most importantly, we deny that we're in denial."

He cleared his throat. "Back then, I only saw what I wanted to see and believed what I wanted to believe, and it worked—especially when I threw some tequila or vodka down my throat. I lied to myself so much that after a while the lies started to seem like the truth. I denied so much that I could no longer recognize the truth right in front of my face." He squeezed her hand and turned his gaze out to the sea. "I learned that you don't drown by falling into the water. You drown by staying there."

An elderly couple passed them and smiled.

Jay stopped walking and turned to her. "I nearly drowned, Christel. And I sunk you as well." He put his arms around her and pulled her in tight.

She looked right up into his face, taking in every word. He said she had a good gut. Her gut was telling her this time he was different.

Jay placed his chin on the top of her hair and whispered in a tear-choked voice. "Please, forgive me, Christel."

33

Christel was not prepared for the wave of emotions that followed Jay's atonement, nor was she expecting the immediate desire that welled inside. She wanted to turn the clock back. She wanted to enfold him in her arms and be one with this man she had loved so fiercely.

Christel recalled what Elta Kané had expressed from the church pulpit weeks back. Love was a tricky word. It was most often understood as an intense feeling of deep affection. Yet, love could have a much deeper and richer meaning, one that transcended a feeling or emotion.

No wonder there were four distinct words in the Bible that defined love. No one word could ever express its entirety.

She put her arms around Jay and felt him lean into her. His emotions were palpable, as were her own. He breathed in and asked what he really wanted to know.

"Christel, do you hate me?"

Tears streamed down her cheeks. How could she ever hate this man who had, and maybe still remained, her soulmate?

All at once, tears rushed to her eyes—tears of deep sadness, confusion, and pain. She felt every beat of her heart, every pulse of blood as it moved through her body. She opened her mouth, but she couldn't, for the life of her, figure out what to say.

For a moment, she couldn't breathe. She felt like someone had pulled the plug on the bathroom drain, like their life together was rushing away in a twirling tornado.

"I could never hate you, Jay," she admitted. "You are—*were*—my life."

The splintered words between them were evidence of so much. They both wanted to understand, they wanted to make the other person feel understood, but the truth was they were on opposite sides of life right now, looking over at each other and imagining what life might have been like if only his addiction had not torn them apart.

His reply was quiet and stoic. "You have a husband."

He looked at Christel, finally, when he said this. Between the look on his face and the way his voice broke when the words seeped from his mouth, she knew that he hated himself for feeling the way he did.

He did this.

There was no escaping the fact that he was responsible for where they were.

Christel's instinct was to grab Jay tightly, to never let him go, to put her hand over his mouth in order to silence the truth. But she knew that even if she could stop the words from coming, that wouldn't make them any less true.

Instead, she took a step back. She breathed in, letting the air in her lungs fill her. "Evan is a good man."

The mood shifted. She could feel it in the air between them. There was no reason to hide what was true in order to cling to what was.

Christel took Jay's hand and brought it to her lips, kissing the warm skin of his open palm. Breathing was taking far more effort than it should.

"Your addiction changed me, Jay. I am no longer the same. While I love you, and always will, I have a new life...a life I love."

It was true. She and Jay were two people who used to be madly in love. But you can't capture love in a bottle. You can't hold onto it with both hands and force it to stay with you. When you are that deeply in love, you're not supposed to be able to love someone else. But she did. She loved Evan.

Jay was looking right at her, listening to every word.

"Evan gave me a gift, Jay...a gift of serenity. Of home." She paused as Jay kept looking at her with his bottom lip between his teeth—the face he made when he was thinking about something hard, turning it over and over in his mind.

Finally, her former husband nodded. His eyes filled with tears and he wiped them with the back of his hand. "I know. I'm grateful you are happy, Christel." His voice choked. "More than you'll ever know."

Christel realized at that moment that they had never had a proper goodbye...this was it.

"I love you, Jay." She leaned and brushed a kiss across his cheek. "I always will."

Then she turned and walked away.

34

Christel let the ocean breeze buoy her spirits as she briskly walked in the direction of the parking lot.

She let images of Evan fill her mind. She could almost smell the laundry detergent on his shirt as she bathed in the knowledge that she wanted to be with him for the rest of her life.

No more unfinished business.

No more uncertainty.

Her mind was no longer struggling with tension, pressure, or confusion. There was simply peace.

It was messy to love after heartbreak. It was painful and it forced her to be honest with herself about who she was and where she'd been. She had to work harder to find words for her feelings because they didn't fit in any pre-fabricated box.

But the struggle was worth it.

Because of where she now was…resting in the security and knowledge that she was where she was supposed to be.

When she got home, she'd tell Evan everything.

Somehow, she believed he would understand. He, no doubt, still harbored love for his dead fiancé Tess, in the deep recesses of his heart. That did not mean he loved Christel any less.

Love was like that...complex and beautiful.

Christel had said goodbye to Jay a million times in a thousand ways. Today was a new way on a new day. A final goodbye. A firm goodbye.

She let the sun warm her face as she played out in her head her need to seal their goodbye.

So long, Jay. It was real, and much of it was good. Now she would continue this new chapter with Evan. She would live her new life with her heart wide open, healed and no longer fractured.

She would think of Jay less even though she might always think of him when she felt the sun on her shoulders. That would always make her think of Jay.

And likely a few times every single day when she wasn't expecting to. That was how it had been, how she suspected it would always be. Because she had been his wife, and Jay was scored on her heart.

But in her heart, she was now married to a wonderful man. Now she was Evan's wife. Every part of her new marriage was as sacred as the one she shared with Jay.

Except, she confessed that she was terrified to love that hard again. Letting go of Jay had changed her. Courage wasn't her fearless go-to anymore. It was the default, the only choice left. If she was going to love at all, she must love well. Loving well was a courageous thing to do.

So, she chose to love again, now fully knowing what it meant to have all her chips on the table. It meant she could lose. But it also meant she could win. Big.

Christel was living a good life, one she never imagined for herself the day she walked out of that attorney's office.

It was a great life. She had a great future ahead. She might even be a mother someday.

A bright smile sprouted on Christel's face as she reached the parking lot. She dug in her pocket for her keys when a voice startled her.

She turned to see Mia standing before her.

"What are you doing here?" Christel asked, not bothering to hide her contempt.

Mia lifted her chin slightly as she leaned against Christel's car and folded her arms. "Observing."

Her heart seized in her chest as she realized that Mia saw her with Jay.

"It's not what you think," she stammered.

Emotion filled her former best friend's face. "It never is."

Mia straightened and turned for her car. As she walked away, Christel grabbed her arm. "Excuse me?" She pointed in the direction of the path. "I don't know what you think you saw, but Jay and I were…"

"You're married," Mia reminded her.

"I know that!"

Mia held up open palms. "Look, you don't have to explain anything to me."

"You're absolutely right I don't. What you saw…what you *think* you saw…was nothing like what you did."

Mia stood there silent. Her pain-filled eyes said everything.

Christel felt a fluttering in her chest and knew it was fear. Mia could turn what she saw all around. She could tell Evan a revised version of the truth.

As if reading her mind, Mia quietly said, "Whatever just occurred is not mine to share."

Relief flooded. "I need to explain…"

In a totally unexpected move, Mia grabbed Christel's hands in her own. "You don't need to."

The silence that followed lengthened. Christel thought of a dozen things she should say right now, but they all sounded trite and stupid in light of her obvious error in judgment. She'd snuck off and met with her ex-husband without Evan knowing. She'd never considered how that might look.

Her choice invited consequences...consequences Mia held in her hand. She had the power to hurt Christel if she wanted.

Perhaps she deserved those consequences. She'd certainly been harsh when wielding judgment on her former best friend when Mia had crossed the line. Yes, Mia's situation was worse. Yet, the bottom line was that a person could believe they are doing the right thing when everything about it was wrong.

She was not wrong to meet with Jay in order to clear up her confusion and stray feelings.

She was wrong not to tell Evan first.

She pulled her hands from Mia's. "What do you want?" Her gaze skittered away, unable to face the woman before her.

Mia cleared her throat. Even so, her voice was choked as she responded. "I want you to forgive me."

The request sunk through Christel, weighing her down.

How could she possibly let go of what Mia had done? She had an affair with her father. She'd crushed her mother's spirit, and splintered their family. The memory of that betrayal was still inside her, protected and cared for through all these months.

"Please forgive me," Mia repeated, her voice barely above a whisper.

How could Christel possibly extend reconciliation after what Mia had done? She not only crossed the line with Christel's father, but she'd stolen him from her. Every time a memory surfaced, Christel stomped on it and told herself Lincoln Briscoe was not the man she thought he was. Not the man who lifted her to his lap and held her when she was afraid. Not the man who pushed her to be anything she wanted.

How could he possibly have loved her and done what he did?

How could Mia?

It hit her then...her conversation with Jay.

People didn't have to stay the same. They got to change. They got to be sorry for what they'd done and make amends.

Alani knew that and had opened her arms to her daughter, leaving the past behind.

Her mother understood and extended her hand to the one who had hurt her. While not forgetting, she embraced the idea that it was not her job to punish the sins of another.

Perhaps it was time for Christel to do the same.

She swallowed...hard.

Then she reached for Mia's hand. "Would you like to go for coffee sometime?" She supposed there was more she could say, something better and more eloquent, more meaningful. Yet, the simple offer was all she had to extend.

Mia looked over at her as if she understood the risk Christel was taking here. "Sure," she said, nodding. "I'd like that."

35

Ava stepped into the grand ballroom of the Wailea Four Seasons hotel. The expansive room was filled with people sitting around linen-covered tables with floral centerpieces and folded cloth napkins.

Her granddaughter spotted her and waved. "Hi, Grammy Ava! We're over here." She motioned across the room to a couple of tables filled with familiar faces.

There was Katie and Jon. Christel and Evan. Aiden and his co-worker, Megan—a sight that brought more than a bit of surprise to her face.

Alani was there with Elta and her son, Ori. Mig and Wimberly Ann, too. Halia Aka and her daughter, Kina, who was Willa's best friend, completed the table.

Her brother, Jack, sat there wearing a black suit...something she hadn't seen before and may never again. He never dressed up that spiffy for her children's weddings. She saw him wiggle his fingers toward a woman at a distant table and tucked that knowledge away for later. Could her brother have a romantic interest developing?

Stranger things had happened.

For example, take the renewed friendship between Christel and Mia. Her oldest daughter was tight-lipped about what had transpired. It didn't matter. What mattered was that Christel appeared to have finally let go of the need to hate Mia and her dad for their actions. Ava hoped that brought healing, as it had in her own heart.

Of course, nothing was more surprising than when her sister announced that she was backing out of her run for state senator. "I only have one opportunity to turn this around with my daughter," she'd explained. "I don't want to mess it up by focusing on the wrong thing."

Tom stood as she approached. "There you are." He leaned and brushed a kiss against her cheek. She sat down next to him, and he squeezed her hand.

Her sister stepped to the podium. She was dressed in a teal blue silk wrap dress and wore their mother's brooch—a pearl and diamond piece their father purchased as an engagement gift for their mother.

The brooch had remained in Ava's jewelry box for years until she saw her sister eyeing it one day. "Do you want this?"

It was hard to extend the offer, but her sister was no longer the spendthrift she'd been. She could be trusted not to sell the piece to cover her mounding indebtedness. In fact, her sister had made many changes. Not only was Vanessa focusing on becoming a better mother, but she and Ava were finally becoming friends.

Vanessa cleared her throat and leaned into the microphone. "Good evening, everyone! Thank you for coming.

My name is Vanessa Hart. I am the Executive Director of Sea Turtle, Inc.. This newly formed non-profit focuses on the rescue, rehabilitation, and conservation of endangered sea turtles on the island of Maui. We're a sister organization and are here to raise funds to support the efforts of the Maui Ocean Center Marine Institute.

She smiled widely out at the audience.

"Let me introduce you to my co-director...my daughter, Isabelle."

Isabelle stepped to the podium, and the two of them absorbed the applause in the room.

Ava couldn't help but smile.

Tom must've noticed. He leaned next to her. "You look happy," he whispered.

She nodded. "I am," she whispered back.

A playful look crossed his face. "Happy enough to go back to my place when this is over?"

Laughter rose through her and spilled out in a light, airy sound of pure joy. "Why, Mr. Strobe, I thought you'd never ask."

EPILOGUE

Aloha! Captain Jack here.

Whoo-ee! I'm sitting here on the Cane Fire, waiting for a bunch of tourists to show and I'm reeling from recent events. Jay showing up on the scene sure was a surprise. Don't you agree? Always liked that boy, but he sure had some demons. Not that I don't imbibe a little now and then! Still, my niece, Christel, struggled a bit as she reconciled her love for her former husband and the decision to move forward with her future.

My sister, Vanessa, also struggled a bit. Ain't it the way it goes? Sometimes, the ones you love most are the impetus for change. Vanessa is a pistol and would, no doubt, have been elected and become our state senator. Instead, she put her kid first. I'm right out proud of my sis.

Now for the news that makes a lump form in my throat.

I had a chat with Kellie (the author) the other day. Know what she told me? She says this next book, Songs of the Rainbow, will likely conclude the Maui Island Series. She is plum tickled with all the emails, reviews, and messages you send telling her how much you've enjoyed making this journey with

Ava and her family. But, as they say, all good things have to end at some point.

The upside is that Kellie plans a Christmas novella called Hibiscus Christmas. Watch for it!

Don't forget to get yourself a copy of Songs of the Rainbow, the next book in the series. (Psst....Kellie says there's a lot of love in the air in this one. Hint: I may just be finding myself a woman!)

'Ole Captain Jack got his copy, and I plan to bury my nose in those pages at first chance. For now, I've got to get back to the dock. Those tourists are anxious to board the Canefire. We're heading over to Pa'ia today. A group of ladies on this trip want to check out all the shops. I don't get the draw, but apparently, the gals like to take home souvenirs and trinkets.

Anyway, grab your coconut bra and grass skirt and hula on over and get a copy of Songs of the Rainbow. I'll catch you later. Aloha!

YES, I WANT A COPY OF THE NEXT BOOK!

A SNEEK PEAK - SONGS OF THE RAINBOW (MAUI ISLAND SERIES BOOK 7)

Chapter 1

Christel and Evan pulled into the main yard at Pali Maui and cut the engine. "Do you have any idea what's up with this family meeting your mom called?" Evan asked.

Christel shook her head. "None whatsoever. She said it was important."

They climbed from their car and waved to Katie and Jon, who were walking their way from the direction of their own house. Willa followed while carrying her little sister, Noelle. "Down. Down. Me want down," Noelle said, wiggling to get out of her sister's arms.

"Fine." Willa sighed with exasperation and lifted the toddler to the ground. Noelle immediately chased after their Cavapoo puppy named Givey.

"Hang onto her," Katie warned.

Willa rolled her eyes. "Of course." She took the little girl's hand. "I live to be Noelle's babysitter."

The comment drew a stern look from her father. He carried a sizeable aluminum pan covered with foil.

Two cars slowly made their way up the long drive. One belonged to Shane and one to Aiden. They pulled to a stop as Ava appeared and stood at her front door. She wiped her hands on a kitchen towel. "There you all are. Come inside. I have a surprise."

The Briscoe siblings glanced at each other and headed for Ava's front door.

Inside, Jon placed the pan on the counter. "Willa made us dinner. Her first attempt at seafood lasagna. She has a real future as a chef," he bragged.

Willa waved off his praise. "Don't go getting all fussy about this until you taste. Like Dad said, it's my first try."

Ava looked at her granddaughter full on, her face painted with a wide smile. "I'm sure the dish will be delicious."

Aiden gave his mother a side hug. "So, what's this little gathering all about, Mom?"

Ava clasped her hands, barely hiding her enthusiasm for what she was about to say. "Well, Alani reached out to me this morning. As you know, Ori has hopes of expanding Ka Hale A Ke Ola. The resource center has been overflowing ever since the big storm. Expansion takes resources...monetary resources. So, we put our heads together."

"That sounds dangerous," Shane teased. He looked down, turning his attention to his baby boy. "Don't eat that!" He quickly bent and pulled Givey's tail from his son's mouth. "Ugh. Carson is at the stage where everything goes in his mouth."

Ava scooped her grandson into her arms and hugged him tight. "I gathered you all to bribe you."

"Bribe?" Katie asked.

"Yes." Ava paused as if considering how to put forth her proposal. Finally, she just said what was on her mind. "We're holding a big talent show and selling tickets. We'll also secure corporate sponsorships. And we're all going to participate."

Christel turned her attention to her mom's boyfriend. "Tom,

why do mothers do that? They tell you what they want as if it's a done deal. No question."

"You're asking me?" he said, laughing. "Have you met my mom?"

She hadn't, but the few things her mother had shared after her trip to Boston had hinted that Tom Strobe's mother was a bit of a control freak.

"So, this is the deal," Ava's face brightened as she passed out papers to everyone. "Here's the list. Christel, you and Evan are going to do a humorous skit. Katie, you and Jon are doing a dance number. Aiden…"

Before she could continue, both her sons held up open palms in protest. "Oh, no. We're not dancing or singing," they said in unison.

Ava parked her hands on her hips. "I have you two lip-syncing an old Carole King song…one of my favorites." She closed her eyes and swayed. "I felt the earth move under my feet."

"Oh, man," Aiden said. "You're going to owe us big time."

"This is for Ori," Katie reminded as she looked down the list. "And all the people who utilize the services at the center."

"Yeah." Willa moved to the refrigerator and got herself a can of soda. "People like Halia and Kina." Her best friend and her mom used to live at the center. They'd met when Willa helped out on a work day.

They now lived with three other women in a loft above a boutique in Pa'ia. One of the women inherited a plot of land nearby, and together, the roommates started a day retreat for women. They called it Banana Patch, partly because of the banana palms on the property and partly after a commune by that name here on Maui that folded years ago.

"Okay, okay," Shane said, folding. "I'm in."

"Me too," Aiden told them.

Ava pulled her two sons into a shoulder hug. "That's my boys."

Aiden's phone buzzed. He pulled it from his pocket and answered, "Yeah. Captain Briscoe here."

Everyone immediately went silent, knowing a call from Maui Emergency Services could mean a rescue was necessary. They all waited and listened as Aiden nodded. "Yeah? No kidding?" He ran his hand through the top of his hair. "I'll be right there."

He clicked off.

"What is it?" Katie asked.

"Son? Everything okay?" Ava added.

Aiden pocketed his phone. "Yeah. I guess. I mean, someone just abandoned a baby at the station."

Evan frowned. "A baby?"

"Yeah. A tiny little girl. Left her in a box on the steps of the station."

YES, I WANT TO PREORDER THIS BOOK!

ACKNOWLEDGMENTS

A special word of thanks to the folks at Maui Pineapple Plantation (waving to Debbie, Lacey, Mary and Ken!) These fine people let me hang with them and see how pineapples are planted, grown and harvested.

Did you know pineapple crowns are planted in the earth by hand? The pineapples take fourteen to fifteen months to grow. Maui is known for wild pigs and if they break through the fencing, they can eat a football field worth of produce in no time.

The Maui Pineapples are picked to order and are the sweetest treat you'll ever pop in your mouth...no, really! I had such a fun time on the tour and learned so much. You guys were so supportive of this series and my heart is filled with gratitude.

Thanks also to Elizabeth Mackay for the fabulous cover designs, to Jones House Creative for my web design, to my editors, proofreaders, and my publishing team, including the fabulous Cindy Jackson. Special thanks to my personal assistant, Danielle Woods. You guys all make this business so much easier, and definitely more fun.

Hugs and gratitude to my best-selling author friend and critique partner, Jodi Vaughn, who made this book so much better.

To all the readers who hang with me at My Book Friends and She's Reading, you are a blast! I can't believe how much fun it is to do those live author chats and introduce you to my author buddies.

Finally, to all my readers. All this is for you!
~ Kellie

ABOUT THE AUTHOR

USA Today Bestselling Author Kellie Coates Gilbert has won readers' hearts with her compelling and highly emotional stories about women and the relationships that define their lives. A former legal investigator, she is especially known for keeping readers turning pages and creating nuanced characters who seem real.

In addition to garnering hundreds of five-star reviews, Kellie has been described by RT Book Reviews as a "deft, crisp storyteller." Her books were featured as Barnes & Noble Top Shelf Picks and were included on Library Journal's Best Book List.

Born and raised near Sun Valley, Idaho, Kellie now lives with her husband of over thirty-five years in Dallas, where she spends most days by her pool drinking sweet tea and writing the stories of her heart.

For a complete listing of books and to connect with Kellie, visit her website:

www.kelliecoatesgilbert.com

ALSO BY KELLIE COATES GILBERT

THE MAUI ISLAND SERIES

Under The Maui Sky

Silver Island Moon

Tides of Paradise

The Last Aloha

Ohana Sunrise

Sweet Plumeria Dawn

Songs of the Rainbow

Hibiscus Christmas

THE PACIFIC BAY SERIES

Chances Are

Remember Us

Chasing Wind

Between Rains

THE SUN VALLEY SERIES

Sisters

Heartbeats

Changes

Promises

LOVE ON VACATION SERIES

Otherwise Engaged

All Fore Love

TEXAS GOLD SERIES

A Woman of Fortune

Where Rivers Part

A Reason to Stay

What Matters Most

STAND ALONE NOVELS

Mother of Pearl

* * *

Available at all retailers

www.kelliecoatesgilbert.com

Made in the USA
Middletown, DE
13 February 2024

49695979R00116